NUTMEG

NUTMEG

Kristin Valla

TRANSLATED BY
JAMES ANDERSON

Weidenfeld & Nicolson
LONDON

First published in Great Britain in 2002 by Weidenfeld and Nicolson
First published in Norway in 2001 by H. Aschehoug & Co. as *Muskat*
Copyright © H. Aschehoug & Co. 2001
This translation copyright © James Anderson 2002

A CIP catalogue record for this book is available
from the British Library.

ISBN 0297 60761 8

Typeset by Deltatype Ltd, Birkenhead, Merseyside
Printed by Clays Ltd, St Ives plc

Weidenfeld and Nicolson
The Orion Publishing Group Ltd
Orion House
5 Upper Saint Martin's Lane
London, WC2H 9EA

His name was Gabriel Angélico and he was born with his heart on the right. All his life he'd lived in the same town, in the same house, in the same invisible speck on the world atlas. As a youth he'd studied Borges and Goethe until he almost went blind, and he had reading glasses before he started university. He was a delicate and sickly child, a friendless soul who did homework for those born under happier circumstances than he. An unremarked shadow that ran through the streets and held its tongue amongst strangers. As an adult though, he grew both tall and sympathetic, a man even the pope would have felt tempted to shower with blessings. But the year his Holiness visited the Andes, when every tenement toilet in Venezuela had his sacred visage plastered up on its walls, Gabriel Angélico sat in his room facing the window, reading. He hated crowds, and seldom went to church, but was easily moved by a well-written novel.

He was five when he discovered that his heart was in the wrong place. His mother had known all along, of course, but she hadn't said anything for fear of making the boy feel even more abnormal than he already did. Instead, it came to his notice in a far crueller manner. He heard it from the lips of a girl. Her name was Flora Fernandez and she was six. In one of their lessons at nursery school the class had to listen to each other's heartbeats, and the honour of placing her ear on

Gabriel Angélico's chest had fallen to a somewhat reluctant Flora Fernandez. Nonchalantly, she clamped her head to the boy's left side, as he sweated incessantly and wrung his hands. She looked up perplexed, and with the candour of a small girl announced:

'But you haven't got a heart.'

The nursery teacher found this odd, but was finally able to establish that Gabriel Angélico did have a heart, it was simply in the wrong place. The university hospital was later to report that not only his heart, but every one of the boy's organs was in the wrong place, as if nature had played a practical joke on him. When just six and a half he was X-rayed from head to foot, and could see with his own eyes that all his internal organs, from his spleen to his liver, were on the wrong side, and that he was nothing less than a mirror image of himself. Gabriel Angélico immediately made up his mind to keep quiet about these irregularities for the rest of his life, in the full knowledge that the outer man was what was important. The only time he ever considered his insides again was when, at the age of eighteen, he signed a document saying that on his death, whether young or old, his body was to be donated to the town's medical faculty, to be used in the interests of science.

Every summer and winter for seven years Professor Angélico sat at the window of the institute where he worked and wondered what one had to do to be liked and respected at the same time. The first thing was an ability to laugh at oneself, as his grandfather Victor Alba had said on one occasion when, during the excusable madness of the Easter festivities, the other children had thrown water bombs at Gabriel

Angélico to make it look as if he'd wet himself. Get in before them and laugh as loud as you can, his grandfather insisted. So, after much brooding, the young Professor had decided to conquer the world with laughter. No one had had the chance to laugh at Gabriel Angélico again, because he always laughed at himself first. Though most students found not the slightest glimmer of humour in verbal paradigms, Professor Angélico's classroom seemed to offer a daily instalment of some South American sitcom. With his doctrine packaged in sophistic commentary, Gabriel Angélico won the attention of his students until, by the end of each semester, he was both loved and feared, abused and admired.

North Americans were the ones who could be charmed most easily. When he began teaching them four years before, he'd looked with wonder on these beings who wore trainers and chewed gum until their jaws fell apart. They'd not seen as much of the world as Gabriel Angélico would have imagined, but they made up for it with an apparent lack of the curiosity so conspicuous in other people. It was here that the Professor's steady mixture of grammar and humour scored its greatest success. Trying to scare North Americans was pointless, since they'd been born with a measure of hauteur and fearlessness towards the world around them. Making them laugh, on the other hand, was a much simpler business. Gabriel Angélico had only to tickle their ears with verbs and conjunctions to teach them Spanish, using throw-away humour as his principal tool.

He wasn't entirely enamoured of his pupils, though. Gabriel Angélico would sometimes forget they were human beings. Then a shadow would pass over his face and remind him of just how much Americans were to blame for the injustices and wrongs in his own native country. He was well versed in the USA's ruthless exploitation of the Latin American continent, and even though he knew that such facts had been played down or covered up in his young students' history books, he couldn't help wanting to hear the occasional self-reproach. Naturally, it was a ridiculous thought. They were appealing youngsters for the most part. Naive, but appealing. They hadn't a clue how to dress, they'd been robbed of all sense of style, but they were friendly and polite enough to listen. A couple of the girls were rather sweet, although they knew little or nothing of the continent on to which they'd just set foot. But he savoured the sight of a slender waist or a newly painted mouth and left it at that.

The whole circus had long become routine. He would begin with the same words every autumn, like the opening of a play that never closed. And so he went on until sometimes he'd wake up in the middle of a line he knew by heart. It never occurred to him that he'd be doing this for the rest of his life, and if he had let such a thought sink in, he might have found it unendurable. Although he was surrounded by people every day, going in and out of doors and up and down stairways, hardly any of them knew him, and Gabriel Angélico realised that there were few individuals in the world he could depend on. Nor did he have any inclination to come into closer contact with the diffuse shadows that made up his surroundings. And so he felt on this morning, too, as he made his way silently across the newly washed lino towards the classroom on the third floor. All he could feel was his school bag's heavy thudding against his thigh and the light thumping of his own heart. Yet again he found himself a prisoner of his own routine, and without anticipation, he entered the room and prepared to inspect his new pupils. The first thing he saw was a small face at the far end of the room. And for once in his teaching career, Gabriel Angélico forgot that vital opening line, only to discover that he'd been treading the wrong boards all his life.

He was the blackest man Klara Jørgensen had seen. She knew Cesar who ran the liquor store in Rio Chico, the fishermen of Vidabella, and daily found herself surrounded by black faces without staring. But never before had she seen a black man wearing khaki trousers and glasses, with the entire Spanish verb system under his arm. He was so tall that he brushed the door lintel as he passed beneath it, and he slammed down his school bag on the desk with such force that everyone thought of the fault-line in the earth's crust which ran through the town. With his tall frame he towered above them all, while they looked back at him from their desks like small mission children. He had a bearing most would have envied, and despite his cheerful expression there was something subdued about his face. His trousers hung loosely about his thighs, and his shirt was as black as the pupils of his eyes. At the sight of him, Klara Jørgensen's face grew hot and her vision fuzzy, and she wondered if she had a cold brewing. She knew she'd never seen him before, that they'd never lived in the slightest proximity to one another and yet there was something in her that seemed to know him. Apart from his erect posture there was nothing unusual about him, nothing of note at all. And yet it was as if everything around them – chalk dust, globes, textured wallpaper – turned indistinct, and in that moment of time he was the only person who existed for her.

5

She'd been everywhere. Even before she'd been born she'd flown to Florence in her mother's belly, in the days when Fru Jørgensen had studied Italian architecture. Klara Jørgensen had come close to being born in an Italian convent hospital, a thought she found deeply romantic. Sadly, she'd had to make do with emerging into the world at Ullevål Hospital in Oslo, in the company of a handful of other infants. But no sooner was she outside the hospital's doors than Klara Jørgensen continued to rove. It could hardly have been otherwise, with a father who was a pilot and a mother who designed houses and decorated rooms and could never get enough of buildings. Klara Jørgensen had been transported to the most far-flung places by train, ferry, Concorde and estate car, but her favourite means of transport was the horse-drawn cab. Her childhood had been tinged with greetings and goodbyes, with dots on the map it would be nice to return to, but that she never saw again. She was a silent girl whose best photographs were in her mind: her father's sheeplike expression after he'd locked the keys in the car in the Nevada mountains, her mother bargaining for silk shawls in a Moroccan market, her elder sister calling to the horses along the highway, and she herself sitting there quietly with her head against the window, watching.

The only concern she caused her parents was that she had a tendency to disappear. When she was five she got separated from her mother at Rome Fiucimino, and it took the airport staff two hours to locate her. They found her in the cafeteria on the first floor with her legs dangling over the edge of a flamingo-red chair as she sat watching the runway. Subsequently they lost her in the gardens of Versailles where she wandered in the surrounding woods, at the Metropolitan Museum of New York on repeated occasions, and in a Canadian residential neighbourhood where she watched lawn-mowing dads through the soft rain of a garden sprinkler. There was nothing unnatural about this as far as she was concerned; once she'd seen enough of one place, she simply moved on to another, and she couldn't quite grasp why her parents looked at her with such anxiety and alarm. Only when she got older did she realise that the most painful thing that can happen to anyone is not to disappear yourself, but to lose a person you're fond of.

As yet, no one she really cared for had gone out of her life. So many people moved constantly through her world, passed in and out of its existential swing-doors, popped up, hurried on, disappeared unnoticed. A very few remained within her ambit. When she was young her parents always held her hand wherever she went, but it was a grasp that gradually loosened, and bit by bit Klara Jørgensen wandered out into the world by herself. The first autumn she spent alone was in Paris, where she circled the Seine while digesting every little alley and drinking lonely cups of coffee in the midst of its bustling street life. After that, she'd travelled by train from one European city to another: Prague, Budapest, Florence and Barcelona, talking to those who approached her, playing cards with a number of passengers, giving away cheap paperback editions of literary classics and receiving others in return. Her father made sure Klara Jørgensen got to the places she had the greatest hankering to see, and for small shards of time, regardless of the season, she disappeared for a few days, weeks or even months. Airports and railway stations seemed to appeal to her most, places where she could stand alone with her destination before her, magnified on massive boards, and know that she was a speck in the huge maelstrom of humanity, shy and insignificant, in a world full of hiding places.

Gabriel Angélico's first thought was that the waiting was over. At the same time he realised that he'd never been conscious of waiting, but that he must have been, because when what you've been waiting for arrives, a piece of mental jigsaw falls into place. The girl was small and delicate, with eyes like glass that changed colour with the light from the window. Her neck was slender and long, her body thin and her chest flat. She had brown hair, but a few tresses had been bleached by the sun. She wasn't beautiful, her face wasn't of the type that automatically demanded attention, but there was an aura of something golden about her that now and again shed its light on his side of the classroom. She didn't look in his direction at all, but stared instead at the mountains outside the window. The gulf between them seemed vast; she sat right at the back, in a light blue dress with shoulder straps and yellow trainers, their laces loosely tied. She had crossed one leg over the other and was carelessly flicking her foot up and down as, with chin propped on hands, she let her eyes narrow to two slits in the light from the window. She had small, pretty hands and wore a silver wrist-watch. Utterly remote from his world, of course.

Gabriel Angélico was convinced he'd never get to know her. He frequently taught students for an entire semester without having a clue who they were. Only the most vociferous and outspoken left their mark in his classes, whilst the rest remained as shadows whose names he could only vaguely recollect. During registration that first day she had calmly raised her hand and wrinkled her lips when he called her name. He'd only used her Christian name, as her surname had a cryptic look about it and contained a letter he wasn't familiar with. Two mornings and four teaching sessions later he'd still not heard her speak or laugh, but only draw back the corners of her mouth in a kind of contemplative wonder at his inanities. He thought that her eyes had a tendency to travel far from what he was doing, as if mirroring something quite different from their surroundings. He never drew her attention, although on the third day he nearly succumbed out of pure inquisitiveness. He almost went over to her side of the room, because just wandering about imagining what her voice sounded like seemed unendurable. But he didn't. She remained dumb and intangible. A face.

The town Gabriel Angélico lived in was long and narrow and lay in a cleft in the Venezuelan Andes. It was a town just the same, with a cinema, a theatre, a cathedral and a library, as well as a museum that housed one of the many swords of the freedom fighter, Simón Bolívar. Its streets all ran downhill and turned to rivers when it rained, while the houses tried to barricade themselves against the torrents of water behind high doorsteps and sharp curb-stones. The air was heavy and polluted from all the cars labouring uphill. Heaps of rubbish gathered by the roadsides, and the trees in the parks grew beards so that in the twilight, they looked like slumbering men. But there were also a number of pleasant little streets that might put the traveller in mind of the Left Bank of the Seine, though the cakes here were much sweeter and the coffee strong enough to wake the dead.

Gabriel Angélico worked at the institute on the town's main avenue, which was conveniently situated next to the airport. The runway could be seen from the classroom window, and every day at 11 a.m. the Professor had to take a short pause while the morning plane from Caracas landed outside. The institute was owned by the American embassy and housed more than a thousand North American university students. It never occurred to him that Klara Jørgensen came from quite another place, even though she seemed a lot more reserved than her garrulous fellow students. Sometimes he found himself inventing a kind of background for her, with a father who was everything from a ship-owner to an editor, and a loving housewife-mother who'd taught her daughter how to dress and keep her back straight when she stood up.

He would observe her as she walked, with her books clasped to her chest and her arms crossed, always wearing a dress or a skirt and with her hair tidily gathered into a pony-tail. She didn't walk like other foreign girls, the ones who always craned forward as if, mentally, they'd already reached their destination. Nor did she make herself seasick on high heels like some little Venezuelan miss, or thrust her bosom or her bottom out, but carried her body just as it was. She didn't appear to have any close friends amongst the students, although he would occasionally catch sight of her in conversation with one or other of them in the institute courtyard. Sometimes she would even open her mouth and laugh without warning. Then Gabriel Angélico would feel a small tug at his heartstrings, because he'd never managed to elicit a similar response from her so far, though it was fast becoming one of his greatest ambitions.

The first written test the Professor set his pupils was thirty exercises on prepositions and irregular verbs. Her handwriting sloped gently to the left with the letters looped together. She had stared down at the sheet in wonder, written without hesitation and been the first to hand in her work. Her answers contained no errors, and it struck Gabriel Angélico that perhaps his classes might be boring her. Her name had been written in block capitals at the top left-hand corner, including that peculiar character in her surname which nurtured the unlikeliest of fantasies concerning her antecedents. At times he would sit pondering where she came from. Possibly she was of Irish descent, like so many others. Perhaps Russian or French. The more he observed her, the more he grew to know her contours, the way she gesticulated as she spoke and opened her eyes wide in amazement. And with each glance he became more and more seduced by the long neck, the slim legs and the thoughtful gaze. When she chanced to look his way, either through the forest of heads above the desks, or from beneath the lemon trees in the institute courtyard, it was as if all life-support systems in Gabriel Angélico crashed and he had to thump his chest to start them up again.

Klara Jørgensen lived in an attic room in a villa close to a beautiful park. The house belonged to a well-nourished lady called Señora Yolanda, who also owned a red scooter and thirty-three cats. Señora Yolanda was Italian but had married a Lebanese man whose name always neatly seemed to elude Klara Jørgensen's memory. He was rarely at home, as his work consisted of travelling round the oil refineries at Punto Fijo where he did maintenance work. To keep herself occupied, Señora Yolanda ran a small restaurant on the ground floor of the house, in an open room with a dirty brick floor that fronted the street. It was a pleasant place, with yellow-checked tablecloths and a bar flanked by high bamboo chairs. A makeshift tiled roof had been erected over the bar, and on the walls hung woven baskets and an oil painting of an Amazonian Indian. The restaurant also employed a taciturn waiter called Mario. A barbecue had been built at the end of the bar and the menu consisted largely of grilled meat and fish. A couple of fans on the ceiling kept the room cool and free from flies.

In the mornings the smell of fried bananas wafted up the side of the house and seeped into Klara Jørgensen's room through its sixteen windows, all of which lacked curtains, so that anyone could look in on the girl. This didn't worry her a bit. On the contrary she liked living at roof level, and she would sit outside her room in the evenings, smoking a cigarette on the stairs. She awoke to the smell of damp cornstarch, fell asleep to a chorus of dogs and grasshoppers, and when she wanted to open a window she couldn't decide which of the sixteen to choose. She ate breakfast and lunch in the restaurant together with Mario, and Señora Yolanda would smile at the sight of the two of them, each sitting so reticently on opposite sides of the table. Of all the students she'd had in the house, the girl was the most unobtrusive. But muted persona apart, her eyes had a life of their own. In the evenings she sat in her room or on one of the rattan chairs in the garden and read one book after another for hours on end, with a questioning look on her face. She always left off reading in the same manner, with a soft sigh and a couple of twitches at the corners of her mouth, before climbing the stairs to her attic room and turning out the light.

Señora Yolanda had a suspicion that the girl felt out of place with all these high massifs about her. Doubtless there were just as many mountains in Klara Jørgensen's native land, but Señora Yolanda thought she seemed to be pining for the sea. On the other hand, she seemed to have settled in well at the school. Every day she'd arrive back with brief accounts of the morning's classes, punctuated with questions about the meaning of certain words and expressions. Initially, her reports came exclusively from the lectures on literature, on Onetti and Cortázar and the small, everyday miracles that were so commonly played out in that part of the world. But gradually she became more and more concerned with grammar, and a certain Professor Angélico, who obviously had a talent for making his students smile. Señora Yolanda didn't know Professor Angélico or his family personally, but she'd heard that several of his female students had fallen for him. When she mentioned this to Klara Jørgensen, the girl's cheeks turned red and she replied that she didn't know the Professor at all, that she'd never spoken to him or he to her, and that she was quite certain he wouldn't recognise her in the street.

Gabriel Angélico knew it was her long before her face was visible. He could tell from her silhouette, black against the afternoon sun, and her light tread on the cobbles. She pressed her books tightly to her chest and walked with small, brisk steps. The willow by the church caressed the cream-coloured benches in the park where she walked, and he knew that they soon would pass one another. In anticipation, he considered whether to smile at her from a distance or wait until she got closer. He wondered if she would show any sign of stopping, or if he should speak first. All this pondering threw him into such a confusion that, when he finally found himself face to face with her, he started. She looked up in surprise, for she had a tendency to stare at the ground as she walked. He smiled, she did the same. A little taken aback, it seemed.

'Professor,' she said in a light voice.

'Miss Klara,' he said.

For an instant she seemed amazed he'd remembered her name.

'Are you taking a stroll?' he asked like an imbecile.

'No,' she replied. 'I've been sitting on one of the benches reading a book.'

He knew that. He'd seen her sit on many benches reading many books.

'Are you enjoying it?' he asked, nodding towards the thick covers she held in her hands.

'It's very beautiful,' she said. 'But I'm afraid I don't understand it properly.'

He became serious and was about to open his mouth to expound.

'Shhh,' she said, laying a finger to her lips. 'I haven't finished it yet.'

By way of reply he smiled again and put his hands in his pockets, something he always did when he couldn't think of anything to say. She, for her part, made a move to continue on her way.

'See you on Monday,' was all she said, and half-turned to take her leave. 'Good-bye, Professor.'

'Good-bye, Miss Klara,' he said.

He didn't dare turn to look at her for fear she might do the same. He couldn't trust himself to continue walking, either. So he went over to one of the benches and sat there with his hands in his lap. There he remained, hoping she wouldn't see him, hoping she wouldn't yet realise just how she made everything swell up and turn sore inside him.

Gabriel Angélico was not a punctual man. He had a habit of arriving late for everything, even his own lessons. But now the dean and the school secretary noticed that not only did he arrive promptly whenever he had to, but he was often there an hour or two before he was due to teach. They both noted this with astonishment, as neither had the least inkling of Gabriel Angélico's admiration for his pupil. The Professor went to bed, night after night, with Klara Jørgensen's face in his mind's eye, and he awoke to the same. Breakfast was completely neglected in his haste to get off. Klara Jørgensen, too, was observed in the school courtyard at times when her attendance wasn't strictly necessary. Each morning she looked quickly at the time-cards as she passed the reception desk. She always noticed if Gabriel Angélico's card had been moved to the other side, and if so, she would glance at herself in the bookshop window and tidy a hair or two. She never looked for him outside the cafeteria, but crossed straight over the courtyard and disappeared into the library to return a book she had finished with. She always borrowed another, and always seated herself on one of the benches outside and began to turn its pages, taking care not to glance over at the other side of the courtyard too often.

Gabriel Angélico would pretend that he was sitting reading the newspaper. In reality he would be studying her minutely over the edge of the page, but he took care to avoid letting her see that his eyes had turned in her direction. This was the sole opportunity he had to observe her, for in the classroom he never permitted his gaze to alight too long on any single face. Day after day he viewed her from afar, like some amorous spy with only the most banal of gadgets at his disposal. He studied her as a painter studies his model. He knew precisely where she would look next, how long she took to read a single page, the way she rested her forefinger against the edge of the book cover. He saw others pass by her from time to time, send her a smile, exchange a few words. He wanted, more than anything, to swap places with them so that he could hear her draw breath for a moment, but he never got close enough. Sometimes he had the impression that she might just as easily have been sitting somewhere else, that in her thoughts she had passed far beyond the fragile boundaries of his own sphere and was wandering in a landscape of which he knew nothing. She had the world in her gaze, mirroring it in her refined subtleties and reflecting within herself the pulse of nature, as if she was on familiar terms with the entire cosmos.

In his blackest moments Gabriel Angélico doubted that they would ever again exchange those chance words that people fire off at one another when they meet unexpectedly. But one afternoon, when he was in the library, she came in through the door, her body swathed in a cloak of sunlight. He started, and felt his breath shorten and his brow become warm. She turned

16

to the librarian and handed in a book she was carrying, and the librarian looked up for a moment and registered its return. Then she turned to Gabriel Angélico and smiled faintly, as a wisp of hair escaped her pony-tail and settled on to her shoulder. He gave a little cough and almost stumbled backwards as she slipped past him. She stopped at the shelf of contemporary Mexican writers and ran her finger over the titles.

'Perhaps you should start with the one you've got right in front of you,' he said, deciding to address her a little less formally.

She turned to him. He pointed.

'That one is very beautiful.'

'But is it sad?'

'Tragic.'

'Fine.'

She was about to take it, but hesitated a second.

'What's it about?' she asked.

'Fate,' he said.

A small furrow appeared in her forehead.

'I don't know a lot about fate,' was all she muttered, before she put the book under her arm and left.

And Gabriel Angélico stood there with a world of hopelessness written on his face.

It was true that the girls whispered about Professor Angélico in the corridors. Not so much on account of his looks, which certainly weren't a lot to whisper about, but because he had a special talent for moving to music. It was dancing that had popularised the silent Professor and made him human. When

Gabriel Angélico was little he'd moved like a toad and talked like a cuckoo and no one had given him a second glance. Then his uncle, the one they called Tio Gordo, taught him to dance the salsa. And suddenly Gabriel Angélico could wiggle his pelvis just like Oscar de Leon the salsa king, and he went on practising in his room to the sound of a slow-running cassette player until he fell asleep from exhaustion. When, at last, he plucked up the courage to venture out of the house with his dance steps, people watched in amazement at how the Professor could move to music. As soon as there was a dance in the town's cobbled market-place, the ladies stood draped along the edge of the bandstand and stared at him with incredulity. And Gabriel Angélico danced until his heart started palpitating and he felt totally worn out. Afterwards he walked home through the sleeping parks with his hands in his pockets.

Only rarely would girls speak of their fascination for the Professor out loud, and Gabriel Angélico himself was unaware of the flutter he caused. However, there had been a couple of exceptions. There was a certain Joan from the English Lake District who, as well as being completely infatuated with the good Professor, also insisted on trying to take him home with her. Lakeland Joan was a lovely girl, if one overlooked her outsized teeth and the rabbit tattooed on her right shoulder. She also had more money than she knew what to do with and immediately hired Gabriel Angélico as a private tutor. Neither the dean nor Gabriel Angélico saw anything suspicious in this, since the Professor hardly had a reputation as a lady-killer. And so he drilled Lakeland Joan daily in irregular verbs, but was forced to admit that, pretty though she undoubtedly was, her attraction for him stopped there. She had no feeling for grammatical analysis and preferred lightweight literature that depicted romance in the most hackneyed tradition. They conversed in the school courtyard from time to time, but no one could have been more surprised than Gabriel Angélico himself when, at the end of the semester, she flourished a plane ticket to London and promised the Professor both a flat and a job in her father's firm.

'Why do you want to take me, Miss Joan?' Gabriel Angélico had asked her.

'Because I like having you around,' replied Lakeland Joan.

But Gabriel Angélico didn't think that a good enough reason to desert his family, and so, with a somewhat embarrassed smile, he politiely declined her offer. Lakeland Joan went about with a disappointed look for a day or two, but recovered with surprising rapidity and placed her affections elsewhere. Not long after, she returned to her lakes in the north, and Gabriel Angélico felt convinced that she had completely forgotten their time together. He alone remembered her offer as he sat by the river feeling the mountains slowly bearing down on him. And then his thoughts might turn to the plane ticket he'd so nearly held in his hand and he decided that, if nothing else, the event had enriched his life. Gabriel Angélico knew now that there was a way out of this rocky fastness, even for him. All he needed was a good excuse to go.

In the shade of the olive tree Gabriel Angélico fantasised about going away with Klara Jørgensen. One day, when he'd plucked up the courage to ask, the dean's secretary had told him the girl came from Norway. As the weeks passed and his fancies grew, the Professor had trouble sleeping at night. He would lie with his hands spread limply on top of the blanket and stare up at the cracks in the ceiling through which the odd insect emerged. He still didn't understand how the evenings could crawl past so slowly. It was as if time had lost all vestige of movement and he was bogged down in some kind of spiritual quicksand. The day's classes were of little comfort. She was so remote she might as well have been mounted in a glass case, like the British crown jewels. He began to pick out the smallest detail about her, the way she became absorbed by what she was reading, the clothes she wore from day to day, the light-blue dress he was especially fond of. So he was all the more amazed when she turned up in the school courtyard one morning, her cheeks flushed by warm winds, wearing a pair of faded jeans with holes at the knees.

'Good morning,' she said breathlessly, halting in front of him.

Gabriel Angélico was so taken aback that he almost mopped his brow with his newspaper. Was she really standing there talking to him?

'You're wearing jeans, Miss Klara.'

'Yes.'

'But you never wear jeans, do you?'

'Don't I?'

'No. Always skirts.'

'You've noticed?'

'Naturally.'

She blushed flatteringly.

'I read the novel you told me about.'

'And how did you like it?'

'It was very beautiful.'

'There, you see.'

'But I'm not sure I understand it properly.'

'That's just the point. Magic realism.'

'Magic?'

'It's not meant to be understood.'

She cocked her head and looked past him, the way she always did.

'May I take the liberty of recommending another book?' he asked.

He handed her a small, dog-eared document that had been in his bag a long time. She peered with surprise at the name below the title.

'Did you write this?'

'Yes. I've been writing it all my life. In fact, I don't know if it's finished.'

'Is it magic, too?'

He smiled, but discovered to his horror that his sight was blurred, as if life had suddenly dealt him a pair of steamed-up spectacles.

'Professor?' she said, looking at him uncomprehendingly. 'Aren't you feeling well?'

The Professor lowered his head and sighed, as if letting out his dying breath.

'Miss Klara,' he said resignedly, 'I believe you are my destiny.'

The words rushed from his mouth like a rockslide and landed heavily on the ground between them. She was still staring blankly at him, unable to grasp the meaning of what he'd just said. Of course she didn't understand. He could repeat it ten thousand times for all the good it would do.

'You can't really know that,' she said almost inaudibly.

'Yes,' he said. 'I've waited for you all my life.'

He looked at her again and Klara Jørgensen felt as if the world had begun to alter about her, as if someone had thrown a transparent cover over it. Gabriel Angélico shot her a look of fear mixed with regret, and her body convulsed in a little shiver. Then he turned on his heel and left. The last she heard was the heavy gate clanging ponderously shut, recoiling from its own weight and banging back again and again, like the impatient heartbeat of the universe.

William Penn lived by the seashore in a white brick house with a veranda. Pot-plants twined around the ropes of the hammock and the windows had shutters and mosquito netting. At the back there was a garden, and to begin with, he had watered the lawn and the clusters of grapes, but eventually he had to give in to the drought, which seemed to last for ever. The beach was constantly encroaching on the grass-covered plain, and by then the garden had long since turned to dust. Instead, he'd acquired a couple of house plants which stood in the shade and didn't get burnt by the sun. For three long years he'd lived there. The residents still remembered the day he'd arrived, minus pot-plants and bearing the smallest bundle of possessions anyone had ever carried with them to Vidabella. Later, they saw him leave each morning for the open sea with a group of tourists in a small sailing dinghy he'd bought and repaired himself. No female company had ever crossed his threshold and he was never to be seen with Divina Fácil and her prostitutes. If he was a solitary man, it was because he chose to be, and it seemed that he preferred meandering along to the sound of his own seclusion. Everyone knew him and they observed him each day with native curiosity. Even so, there was no one who could claim to know who he was.

Just as a chameleon changes colour according to its surroundings, his humour would alter depending on who he was with. Nothing appeared to irritate William Penn, because in the course of his thirty-four years he'd learnt that irritation was a useless thing to waste one's time on. Instead, he conversed with one and all, sat on street corners and in seamen's bars into the small hours talking about Southern Ocean winds and village politics. His amiability was all-embracing, even the stray dogs allowed the Captain's strong hands to stroke them. No one who crossed William Penn's path could fail to feel a certain attachment to him, neither the fruit vendors, nor the *empanadas* women nor the gaggle of tourists he sailed with every day during their short holidays. People had got used to seeing him on his days off, sitting at a rickety table beneath the grape-trees. There he would chat to anyone who passed by, and most of them would come up and join him when they saw William Penn sitting there with a cigarette. No one had any idea how he'd landed up on the island or what hopes he nurtured for his future there. But it was clear to all that he was a seaman, though his language wasn't particularly coarse and there were no pictures of females etched on his arms. But when evening fell and the Captain eventually turned in, everyone could see that William Penn had life tattooed on his face.

After two years a girl appeared. She came from nowhere with her large suitcases and over-warm clothes, and people thought she must have fled from winter because she was as white as the ocean foam. There was little doubt that the Captain was a good deal older than her, because whereas she had skin that was as smooth as a sea-honed stone, his face was full of deep wrinkles. His hands were hard and dry, and he would sometimes get large cracks in them that ran from the knuckles and disappeared into his broad palms. The locals would gaze inquisitively after him as he put his great arm around the girl during their quiet conversations beneath the grape-trees. There was an accustomed intimacy between them, and the secrets they whispered to each other were shrouded by Caribbean winds. Their relationship appeared to be founded on something quite different to Latin love, which so quickly turned tepid. On the contrary, what these two shared looked to be anything but transient, and seemed to be based on a friendship of the deepest kind. William Penn might have been a seaman, but on land he sometimes looked quite lost. He could navigate his way across the oceans of the world using the planets and constellations, but as soon as he arrived in port he couldn't tell right from left, and he allowed himself to be piloted by the girl.

Her name was Klara Jørgensen and she was twenty-one. William Penn hadn't known her long, but even so he'd learnt to read every sign in her occasionally enigmatic looks. When a thing troubled her, she would furrow her brow into deep wrinkles, like a wind raking formations in desert sand. If she felt inquisitive, her eyes would grow large in her face like saucers. At other times sadness would descend over her features like a soft shading, and he was the only one who could read it in her face. He'd never seen anyone cry like Klara Jørgensen. Tragedies might unravel before her and her eyes wouldn't even become moist, but then she would burst into tears over the smallest things. It took time to understand this, how she saved up her tears and then let them flow at the oddest times. She never cried in front of anyone but him; it was only William Penn who would hear her sudden sobbing and know that she was really crying for all the butchered chickens at the market, the lemonade-seller's dead son, the thirsting trees, or the fact that she periodically felt herself friendless.

The people of Vidabella had long got used to the sight of the two of them. They'd become a part of daily life, whereas the tourists hurried past with sun hats and sparkling towels, full of vim and factor fifteen. People no longer noticed her clumsy Spanish as she haggled for squid, or the Captain's affectionate treatment of her. In small-town Santa Ana one seldom reflected on whether people had come to stay or not. When you'd seen them more than twice they were part of the general scene, like flies in a window-sill or grains of sand in the market-place. The Captain and his girl were now even mentioned outside the liquor store on Sunday mornings, as if her presence had turned the Captain into more of a fellow creature. Umberto the barman, one of the few on the island with a genuine nuclear family, used to say that if one thing was certain, it was that William Penn loved Klara Jørgensen. Umberto used to say it to the girl too, but she would merely smile and turn her face to the breeze. 'I know that already,' she might reply, and Umberto the barman would nod. Everyone could see that the Captain loved her. But no one had ever heard him say so.

Not far from the Captain's beach house, Ernest Reiser awoke to the face of his loved one. She smiled at him in all her unsullied beauty with a face that might have bewitched an entire world. Her cheeks had little dimples that ran to the corners of her mouth and her eyes slanted gently up towards her dark hairline. Her hands rested serenely in her lap, doll-like and pure, with fragile nails and soft palms. The photograph was thirty years old and had been taken in one of Geneva's parks in late summer. She was dressed in a white cotton frock, a blinding contrast to the dark skin that announced her origins to all and sundry. It was still how he remembered her, though lines had long since spread, net-like, over her skin. There were many other times he'd seen her sit just like that, but now it was with back bowed and wrinkled hands, and hair that turned greyer each moment he looked at her. Not in a park, as then, but at a wobbly table before a draining-board with stains on her dress and laddered nylons, which she kept washing because she didn't have the money to buy new ones. And yet this was the picture he always carried with him. Not the woman life had made her, but the young girl full of newly discovered beauty, who had enraptured him from the first moment she'd sailed into his world.

It was long since and it was only a moment ago. Ernest Reiser got up and sluiced a bucket of water over himself with his door ajar. It was five in the afternoon. He coughed as if hawking up his entire chest and dried himself with weary movements. He was a small, dishevelled man, thin as a pea-stick and wrinkled as a bloodhound, with a stomach that was hollow at times. But his appearance was immaculate, he was always punctilious about having his beard trimmed by the same barber, and no one could accuse him of not wearing socks. Ernest Reiser still had something of the European about him, although he no longer bore the stamp of any particular nationality, but appeared to have been branded by a number of cultural irons. In his youth he'd been what people call up-and-coming, a gifted man, fluent in French and English, who also took pride in being able to speak High German like they did on television. In those days he moved in refined social circles, he went to parties, bought silk shirts and had his suits made to measure. Ernest Reiser could tell one wine from another just by tilting his glass, spout phrases about music and politics and treat a woman so that she felt like a real lady. Once he'd flown right round the world and been served champagne both on take-off and landing. Then the whole thing came to an abrupt end. All because of a woman.

He'd seen her dusky face fill a Swiss assembly hall on that occasion thirty years ago. He had immediately crossed the floor to meet her. He'd given her a glass of something bubbly and tried to get her talking, in the hope that they spoke the same language. When she stared uncomprehendingly at him, he immediately switched to French, and so they began a conversation. But she only told him where she came from and little more, a land far to the west that he'd never heard of, a sun-scorched, equatorial country of coffee plantations and uninhabited jungle and a coastline strewn with mini-paradises. She left him with these images of her country and turned down all his subsequent invitations. It was only after weeks and months of orchids, chocolate hearts, opera tickets and expensive dinners, that he finally won her. They were married in a simple ceremony in the park outside the Venezuelan Embassy. Shortly afterwards Ernest Reiser set his over-insulated feet on the South American continent for the first time and gazed with wonder at the windswept trees on the Maiquetía coast and the mud huts huddled one above the other on the hillsides.

His meeting with Caracas was like a small slap in the face. He couldn't get used to all the crime and poverty, never being able to take a walk through the streets in the evening, but always having to drive from door to door and lock the car away in subterranean garages, and then seek refuge in one's own living-room. Two of his neighbours were shot during his first year there, even though his home lay in a very respectable district. That first year he worked at the embassy on the same side of town, but after a while his job was axed and he had to look for other employment. He seemed to be incapable of making his wife pregnant and her family looked upon this disconcerted European, who was steadily sliding down the wage scale, with a smidgen of contempt. At last they had to move to a cheaper part of town, where the nightly noise and his wife's constant complaints began to drive Ernest Reiser mad. And so love died, just as prayers do when they're never answered. Finally, Ernest Reiser packed his second-hand suitcases and went to a small island nobody had heard of. Here he began to cultivate his beard and his sarcasm, forced to spend his remaining years in a shabby restaurant facing the world's loveliest sunset.

Each evening Klara Jørgensen sat waiting for the Captain. She drank a lemonade through two straws and stared at closely printed pages to the sound of waves lisping on the shore. She smoked one Blue Belmont, the Venezuelans' own tobacco which they grow at the foot of the mountains, but never more than one, and she was always alone. Nor did she seem to take any notice of her surroundings, the deserted restaurant tables, the threadbare tablecloths with stains that would never come out, the sooty ashtrays and the cracking plastic chairs. Even the fêted sunset went unnoticed. She was totally lost in what lay between the covers she held in her hands. The barman Umberto and the waitress Bianca Lizardi never approached her when she sat like this, for they felt she was trying to make herself invisible there on the chair. Even so, Klara Jørgensen had long since become part of the ritual that unfolded on the beach in the evening hours. Ernest Reiser appeared in the doorway with great sweat marks on his chest and cursed softly in three languages. As the manager of the place he claimed the right to bemoan its lack of clientele, even though the regulars would soon come slinking in out of the darkness.

The restaurant's owner arrived in a blue pick-up and parked by the door of the stationer's shop which was still festooned with Christmas decoration, though it was well into August. Henrik Branden was a Norwegian and had been a lorry driver in his native land, but he'd fled from four speeding fines on a standby ticket to a Caribbean paradise and had subsequently struck gold. The chain that nestled amongst the hairs of his chest was made from finds in the rivers of El Dorado, as was the ring on his little finger and the décor on his spectacle frames. The run-down restaurant on the beach which he owned earned him no money. It simply satisfied his insatiable need for cheap rum. Henrik Branden went straight to the far end of the bar and without a word, Umberto placed the first *cuba libre* of the evening on the table in front of him. The Norwegian felt the ice-cold liquid filter into his blood, like a moist sponge on a sunburnt brow, bringing with it a mild sting in the chest.

A woman came in and seated herself next to Henrik

Branden. Carmen de la Cruz resided with him in his polyester palace on the eighth floor of the Residencias el Griego. She looked older than her forty-six years, but then she'd done more living than most people. It was said of Carmen de la Cruz that in her time she had been both a prostitute and a dealer in stimulants, and for those who gave her a cursory glance it wasn't hard to believe the truth of such rumours. Ernest Reiser was in the habit of saying that the dress-making trade saved money when it made clothes for Carmen de la Cruz, as not a lot of material was required. She had ample curves, a cleavage so deep that the locals christened it the Valley of Delight, and a number of indelible artworks tattooed on her shoulders and thighs. Her hair was heavily bleached, her mouth puckered from years of smoking and her voice resembled that of a seasoned old tar. Her speech was peppered with oaths and she laughed like a landslide, and when she smiled, it was only to expose a very depleted row of dirty yellow teeth.

Bianca Lizardi contemplated her boss and his other half by the gleam of the lanterns. The tall Norwegian was attractive and she wasn't unmindful of his financial status. He didn't look too bad at all, although he'd obviously go bald one day. Bianca Lizardi had no plans to remain a waitress for the rest of her life. Privately, she groomed herself for a more elevated social position; she bought expensive fashion magazines with the money she earned and had picked up enough English to converse politely with the visitors. She had an alluring appearance, and was so slenderly built that she sometimes looked like a girl, but with an air that would have made even a poisonous snake bit its own tail. If Bianca Lizardi's admiration for Henrik Branden was something she kept to herself, her contempt for Carmen de la Cruz was unmistakable. The two women had never exchanged a single word, despite their close proximity in the restaurant for much of the day. Bianca Lizardi had no time for bread-and-butter whores like Carmen de la Cruz, as she emphatically stated, with their uncensored fantasies and over-fragile principles. True, she brought them what they wanted in the way of food and drink, but no one could make Bianca Lizardi talk to them.

There was a slight fretfulness in the air, as if a thunderstorm was about to come sweeping in from the Caribbean. A pelican flew into a cliff. Klara Jørgensen looked up for a moment and winced at the red light on the line of the horizon. Suddenly she began to feel chilly sitting there.

'Pelicans hurl themselves at the cliffs when they get old,' said Ernest Reiser, who had noticed her astonishment.

'You mean they commit suicide?'

'No, they resign themselves to death. That's something rather different.'

On the horizon she caught sight of the dark outline of a sailing boat approaching. Soon she expected to hear the rattling of the anchor chain and the oars of the rowing boat smacking the surface of the water. But there was something in the air, an oppressive, audible signal, a shimmering warning that kept growing in intensity. She put her book down on the table and turned to the people behind her. They had heard it too, for Henrik Branden rose and looked out through narrowed eyes.

'The sound of an accident,' he muttered and went down towards the beach.

A lone tourist came rowing in at breakneck speed with his oars squealing in their locks. As soon as he was close enough he jumped overboard and swam in as best he could, against tide and gravity, driftwood and pieces of torn fishing net. He panted as he dragged his dripping body up towards the rickety restaurant tables. His hands shook and his eyes wandered wildly about.

'Call a doctor,' he gasped.

He spoke in Danish, and then repeated the sentence in English. Those present could only stare at him as he stood there with his back bent, hands on knees, like a footballer who has lost time and time again. Ernest Reiser placed a blunt finger in the dial of the phone and waited.

'The doctor's at the brothel. The ambulance is on its way,' he said at last.

Bianca Lizardi lifted an eyebrow and tried to imagine the good doctor between the sheets at Divina Fácil's.

'What happened out there?' Henrik Branden asked the pale tourist.

'He was swimming and suddenly he was dead.'

Klara Jørgensen got up. The book fell to the cold stone floor. By the wall of the house the fishermen's catch lay belly up in scarlet sand. A stray dog howled out its hunger. She saw a small fishing boat making its way in towards land. Across its thwarts was a door, and on the door, a man. Klara Jørgensen recognised the door. She'd seen the commissioner sleep on it

33

when she'd accompanied them to the small islands. He liked to fish and occasionally to spend the night out there, and the door protected the commissioner from ants and other creepy-crawlies while he slept. Now it had become a stretcher. Two figures were bent over the lifeless body that lay there. One was the commissioner. The other was William Penn. They made alternate attempts to blow some life into the dead man.

William Penn didn't notice her as she came wading out. He was on his knees in the boat, crouched over the inert form. It was that of a young man dressed in mauve bathing shorts. His skin was turning violet too, the muscles of his face had gone limp, his eyes had stopped moving. Behind the young man's half-open lids two empty pupils were all that remained, as if someone had gouged his eyes out of his head. The Captain bent down to the young man's lips and blew. White froth and small pieces of meat emerged from the corners of his mouth. The commissioner wiped the victim's face with a coarse piece of cloth. People came wading out from the beach, leant on the side of the boat and stood draped around it like passive film-extras. William Penn cursed softly, partly in Spanish, partly in Norwegian, lowered his mouth and blew again. Yellowish green acid came oozing up from the boy's stomach, and the Captain's face contorted as he turned aside and vomited. Quickly, he passed a hand across his face and carried on. He wiped away the froth from the boy's jaws and bent down towards the smell of beer and yeast, meat and salt. No one knew how long he'd kept it up. No one checked the time, and no one made to leave. But for an instant Klara Jørgensen raised her head and looked at the sleeping fishing smacks, the sinking sun that etched a bloody tinge on the horizon, the shadows in the sand, a flickering street light that was about to expire. So this, thought Klara Jørgensen, is what it looks like when God takes a human life.

Two ambulance drivers arrived and spread a sheet over the youth's face. They placed him on a stretcher, pushed his passport into his pocket and drove him away. The boy was Norwegian and twenty-five years old. He'd been on holiday with his fiancée. Now the girl stood with her head against a gnarled tree trunk, sobbing. She was alone, though maybe she hadn't realised that yet. A police inspector was trying to talk to her, but she just hid her face and wept. The tourists on the promenade stood with bowed heads as if rain was dripping on them. Darkness had long since eaten up all details of the landscape, and only the lamps from the restaurant cast light on the flat stones. Ernest Reiser stood in the doorway with folded arms, watching it all. From his expression it was impossible to guess what he was thinking, but there was a trace of recognition about his eyes, as if he'd lived too long to let himself be moved by such a sight. Calmly, Ernest Reiser let his gaze dwell on the dead man's fiancée, who hid behind her black hair as she pressed her face to the bark. Perhaps he was wondering if there was anyone left who would cry like that for him.

William Penn knelt in the sand looking out towards the horizon. His hands lay in his lap, his chest heaved and sank as if he was straining to breathe. Now and then a dribble of yellow ran from the corners of his mouth and he raised a hand to wipe it away, lowered his head to spit, before he looked out at the sea once more. His eyes were slits, as if they were trying to penetrate the rift between sky and sea far out there. Where he sailed every day, where he loved to sail, his domain. But now he knew that he'd never again forget the taste of half-digested food. Never again be able to eat from that barbecue without knowing the taste of death. He had been dealt a stinging wound, into which fear would dig her long fingernails.

Klara Jørgensen stood before him with feet apart. She stood mute and motionless before the weary Captain. She felt ill. Her fingers quivered like small flames in a draughty room and her eyes had a glassy expression. With something akin to effort she lifted a single forefinger and placed it on the Captain's bowed neck. He sighed as he fumbled to find her thighs. And so he steadied himself as he rested his forehead on the girl's bare stomach. They stayed like this without speaking. The waves drowned their breathing and he clutched her legs so tightly that she thought of bruises. Klara Jørgensen sank down on the sand in front of the Captain.

'I thought it was you,' was all she said.

'I know,' he replied.

'It could have been you,' she said.

'It could always be me,' he answered. 'It's the same for all of us.'

The body of the dead tourist was loaded on to a charter plane together with fifty suitcases and an empty birdcage. His fiancée sat on the plane by an empty seat and cried her way through two variations of grilled chicken, six time zones and a bad feature film. The coffin was watched silently by one or two fellow passengers as it was transported to the plane. The cabin crew said little or nothing. It wasn't the first time they'd witnessed someone being snatched away like that, and even if it didn't happen right in their back yard, they would usually recognise the corpse in the capital's daily newspaper. Most of them lost someone here and someone there, an uncle of seventy, a cousin of ten, the woman at the laundry might vanish one day and it wouldn't occur to anyone to ask where she'd gone. That was how it had always been – some people disappeared, others arrived in an equally inexplicable manner. In this part of the world death was as commonplace as life itself.

Klara Jørgensen stood with her arms folded on the first floor of the Aeropuerto Francisco Miranda, next to an automatic orange-squeezer. She looked out at the runway, at the coffin being pushed into a headwind, at the airport staff shoving it before them, their backs bent, at the passengers who stood waiting. She thought they seemed foreign, with their earrings, their handbags and sunglasses. Quite unlike herself. They had come here to visit and now they were returning, to a place she too called home, but a home she couldn't really feel with her body. Over the Atlantic somewhere, beneath the same blue vault of sky, her father was weeding the flowerbeds on his few days off and trying to coax her sister into going for a walk with him in the forests around Oslo. Over there, her mother was drawing lines and levels, building on to a world which was already complete in comparison with what was here. It had reading rooms, galleries with paintings one could admire any old Wednesday afternoon, tram lines, seagulls and autumn dusk. Klara Jørgensen had long since weaned herself of all these. She wasn't a person to suffer from homesickness. Her thoughts seldom revisited the places she left. And yet, suddenly, she discovered she was standing there with something like a longing, because she didn't know when she would go back. She had a return ticket, but it was undated; it lay in her bedside drawer, beneath crumpled postcards, photos and newspaper cuttings her parents had sent her, as if in reality it would never be used.

She went downstairs, among shops which all sold the same souvenirs, a coffee bar that tried to look European, and the airline desks at which tickets were sold for half a Venezuelan monthly wage. An accustomed chaos reigned, in which no natural order had ever been able to establish itself, as if they all were dependent on a certain disorder to survive. She was almost bowled over a couple of times, because she looked at the ground too much as she walked. The departures board announced the destinations in white letters: Valencia, Barquisimento, Maracaibo and Cuidad Bolívar. And a small place up in the mountains she'd never heard of. There was a picture of it on the wall, a town surrounded by 13,000-foot masses of stone, well hidden in a cleft of the Andes. It was served by only one flight daily, a twenty-seater propeller plane that hugged the mountain so closely that one could pick out the mule tracks on the plateaux. Klara Jørgensen sat there studying the picture of this landscape, with its sudden tropical vegetation in the high mountain terrain, its low brick houses, cobbled streets and small men in cowboy hats. It was nothing like the Venezuela she knew, there were no arid plains or somnolent sandy beaches, no humid sea breezes or cactus-covered bluffs. Just mountains, vast mounds of rock, high above the rain forest and savannah. Klara Jørgensen looked around at everything that had become known and familiar, at these faces she'd seen time and time again, the same words, the same gestures and the air which never seemed to change. She hadn't packed her suitcases for a very long time and it was as if she began to itch inwardly. Slowly she got up from the chair and went to one of the desks.

'A ticket to the mountains, please,' she said.

'Certainly,' said the woman. 'And when would you like to travel?'

'As soon as possible.'

'Do you want a return ticket?'

'Yes. But leave it open.'

The woman looked at her over the rim of her glasses.

'Of course, I can't guarantee a departure,' she said.

'No, of course not.'

Klara Jørgensen nodded, for she knew already that in this part of the world no one could ever guarantee anything at all. She reached over to the counter and took a brochure that contained a picture of the place. It seemed small and secluded. With a tiny smile she took the ticket and put it in her pocket together with the brochure. Without another thought about what she'd done, she climbed into the car and began to drive homewards.

In the evening she sat on the beach and listened to the sea. She thought the sound seemed hollow and unremitting now, like a rushing, a separate sphere, the very sound of the earth's core. The waves scudded across the world's surface with their white foam and gave life, took life, swept along fishing nets, pelicans, messages in bottles, salt and death. These breakers had lulled her to sleep at night, but now they kept her awake. The noise of them filled her with anxiety, it was as if she couldn't bear to have it outside, the mighty sea that could swallow a person in a moment and then wash away all trace. On the table in front of her lay Horacio Quiroga's stories about love, death and madness. She hadn't opened the book that evening; instead it had been pitted by the sand grains on the tablecloth. Now and then she scanned the horizon and waited for the slightest sign, a mast, the billowing of a sail. When there was nothing, she peered instead at the brochure she held in her hands, at the pines and palm trees that grew side by side and the people with their jackets over their arms in case the evening turned chilly.

'Is that Norway?' asked Umberto, as he waddled past.

'No,' she said without glancing up. 'It looks a bit like your home and a bit like mine.'

'Where is it?'

'Not far from here.'

As William Penn came wading in towards land, she stood at the water's edge waiting. He smiled at her from a long way out, and his smile grew larger as he drew nearer. She looked at his long arms, the arms that held her each night, that never released their grip, never got tired or went to sleep. The hands that were large, but that always touched her gently. As he walked towards her now, with the weight of his years and experience, she had a sudden moment of uncertainty and knit her brows.

'What are you thinking about, Klara?' he asked.

She smiled at him.

'I'm thinking that you're hungry,' was all she said.

He placed a cold hand on her right cheek and kissed her

other one. Together they walked to the grape-trees and he began to wash his feet. The tourists trooped past in a silent band and he said goodbye to them one after the other. Stray dogs gathered round the remains of the barbecue and fought over some scrap of chicken bone. Klara Jørgensen installed herself in the restaurant once more, and shortly after the Captain came and joined her. He ordered his usual rum and lit a cigarette as the water dripped from his bathing shorts and ran down the chair-legs.

She had made up her mind.

'There is something,' she said.

'What is it, Klara?' he said.

'I'm thinking of travelling.'

He gave her a surprised look.

'You'd like to leave?'

'Yes.'

'You want to go home?'

'No.'

'So where were you thinking of going?'

'To the Andes.'

'And how long do you intend to be away?'

She smiled softly.

'For a while.'

The Captain smiled back and laid his hand on top of hers.

'Then I'll miss you,' he said.

'And I'll miss you,' she said.

'But you're still going.'

'Yes.'

He nodded slowly as the ash from his cigarette fell on his thighs, and stuck there.

41

'It must be boring for you,' he said.

'I've been here a long time now,' she said.

'Eighteen whole months.'

'An eternity.'

They both chuckled.

'And you, Captain? How long will you sail these waters?'

He smiled.

'For a while.'

He let his gaze drop to the water's surface.

'It won't be the same,' he said. 'Nothing will be the same without you.'

'I'll be back,' she said simply, sure of her own words.

A lone tourist stood by a crooked tree on the beach and tried to photograph the sunset. A tiny human being's attempt to capture something greater than himself. Klara Jørgensen and William Penn had long since realised the futily of such experiments. She glanced up at the Captain as he rose against the fiery background.

'I'm going to make tracks,' he said and lit another cigarette. 'Are you coming?'

'In a moment.'

He nodded and vanished in the clouds of cigarette smoke that so often shrouded his departure. Soon his body had been turned into a dark outline by the dusk. She picked up the book which lay on the table in front of her, and which she still hadn't touched. Even now she didn't read much before pushing it away again, twitching the corners of her mouth.

'Don't you like it?' asked Umberto behind her.

'It's beautiful,' she said. 'But impossible to understand.'

Then she put down five hundred bolívares on the grubby tablecloth and left to follow a shadow on the shore.

The house in which Gabriel Angélico lived was draughty and stood down by the river. It was his mother's and she, in turn, had been given it by her dear, devoted parents. Ana Risueña was a beautiful woman with a tired face. She had great bags under her eyes, filled with troubles only she knew the depths of. But when she smiled, wrinkles of pleasure spread across her whole face, like the many tributaries of the Orinoco on the map of Venezuela. The Professor's mother had a generous bust and a capacious stomach, but her legs were thin and age had made her skin pale, almost transparent. When she spoke, it was with such serenity that her words immediately spread their roots in the memories of her listeners. In former years, she'd devoted herself to painting, but had quickly realised that this was no way to get rich. And rich she'd never become; her son had long since taken over the role of breadwinner for both his mother and sister. The only testaments to Ana Risueña's talent were the paintings, small canvases in heavy wooden frames, that decorated the family's living-room.

The river below the house was overgrown and impenetrable, covered with sleek growths that spread across the water like the skin on a cup of warm milk. Outside the house there were two lamps flanking the door, the warm glow from which attracted frogs and water-cockroaches. Gabriel Angélico and his sister would sit under the olive tree on cool evenings and contemplate ragged water-lilies and labelless bottles drifting past. They nodded to people who came by, neighbours who halted to relate some story or other and then wandered on into the obscurity of the riverbank. This was a very different Professor Angélico to the one who daily presented himself at the institute. His reading glasses and trousers had been exchanged for shorts and sandals, and he never once tried to elicit a smile. He didn't smoke or drink, unlike most people who made up this small community. Nor did he read, but just sat contemplating. Later, when it was cool inside, he would get out his books and sit down facing the window to write in his room, in a swarm of bewildered night moths.

After that fatal day in the school courtyard, Gabriel Angélico had sat at table every evening glancing furtively at the vacant fourth chair. He tried to think of Klara Jørgensen seated there, with her fair hair and her wondering eyes turned on him. If he stared long enough he almost managed to conjure up a picture of her sitting on the chair, in her light-blue dress and the shoes that she sometimes forgot to lace up, gazing out of the window with that far-away look. And on each occasion he realised how impossible it would be to make her part of his life. This notion was confirmed by the sight of his mother, who would appear with a greasy apron and a face wet with steam. Even his sister was like most of the young girls of the place, totally uninterested in anything beyond the confines of this town that the mountains had swallowed, as if God had shut his fist around it so that no one could get away.

With much effort he managed to get up on Monday morning. Just how he'd be able to meet her gaze, he had no idea. Perhaps she'd been scared or simply insulted – how could he tell? Perhaps she'd content herself by staring at him curiously with that look she fixed firmly on the most diffuse prospects. It would be unendurable, whatever happened. He should have kept his mouth shut, or at least phrased things differently. How could he possibly explain to her the mysterious lines of destiny, drawn like a map in the human heart? How could he convince her that they were fumbling about in this same turbid reality, the one in search of the other? She would never believe him. And before he had clocked in, with a nod in the direction of the secretary's sleepy face, Gabriel Angélico had made up his mind to do both himself and Klara Jørgensen a favour. He would never speak to her again.

Klara Jørgensen stood on the pavement in a cascade of light by a white garden fence. She was wide awake and had the feeling that she'd never need to sleep again. The grass in the park was covered in dew, as if the earth had wrung the moisture out of its very core during the night. A *tigua* by the wall scattered yellow flowers, and the air was heavy with pollen. Like a many-shaded orange carpet, the leaves covered the asphalt, and the morning sunlight was mirrored in the attic windows. The roofs had taken on a golden hue, a fairytale landscape of gutters and tiles. She stood there feeling the vibrations from the treetops and the wingbeats of the birds. The smell of birch bark and green grass mingled with the faint scent of oranges, and she thought she could hear laughter from above, as if someone was expressing joy on her behalf. But all she saw when she raised her head were the ancient telephone wires and the ice-blue sky above.

She glanced down and discovered she was wearing her slippers. With a smile she picked up the newspaper and padded through the back yard and into the garden. Señora Yolanda was seated on a white painted chair in the shade with some knitting in her lap. Klara Jørgensen stood hesitating by the garden table, while a three-legged cat rubbed itself against her ankles.

'Señora Yolanda,' she said at last. 'What do you know about Professor Angélico?'

Señora Yolanda continued her knitting, but looked as if she was considering the matter. She had heard a thing or two about the Professor, in amongst the usual tittle-tattle of the neighbourhood women.

'There have been girls who've tried to tempt him away from here. But he wouldn't go.'

Klara Jørgensen's brow showed a small furrow.

'Hasn't he been anywhere?'

Señora Yolanda smiled.

'People here don't travel much,' she said.

'But your husband travels, doesn't he?'

'He doesn't travel. He works.'

Señora Yolanda sighed with a hint of indulgence.

'Remember, Miss Klara, that travelling means moving from place to place as the fancy takes you and never calling anywhere home.'

'Yes, that's true.'

Then Señora Yolanda's eyes widened as a thought struck her.

'They say he was born with his heart on the right.'

'Professor Angélico?'

'Yes.'

'Is he ill?'

'No, it works just as well on the right as on the left.'

Klara Jørgensen was startled for a moment and felt her own heart, to make quite sure it was on the correct side of her body. It beat gently, she could barely feel it through the fabric of her blouse, but it seemed to be bigger, as if it had grown a bit in her chest overnight.

'Señora Yolanda, do you believe in destiny?' asked Klara Jørgensen.

'No,' said Señora Yolanda.

'Why not?'

'One mustn't expect too much from life,' was Señora Yolanda's reply.

Then she gazed up at Klara Jørgensen's smooth face and added.

'Everything is such a lottery.'

In the school courtyard Rosa Rama had put the virgin out for the day. She got the morning coffee ready and then began to wash the floors. The gilded Virgen de Fatima had a halo on her head and a bowl for coins at her feet. By the end of the day the bowl was always full, and even some of the students were drawn to the jingling prayer for God's much-sought-after intercession. In all innocence, Rosa Rama herself threw five centavos into the bowl and crossed herself before going on with her mopping. She arched her eyebrows sceptically as Klara Jørgensen hastened past, insensible to all higher powers. The girl was hugging her books to her chest again, as if to muffle the sound of her own heartbeat, and was hurrying up the stairs to her classroom. Everything was as normal. Gabriel Angélico stood before the blackboard, his back toward her. He stood towering there as before, with his long fingers that never did anything but leaf through books. Klara Jørgensen froze in the doorway and felt her chest begin to expand. She started to feel unwell, as if she was incubating something her body wouldn't tolerate. Gabriel Angélico hadn't seen her arrive, but he was sure she was there. She didn't move. He turned slowly. For an instant they looked at one another, each more distant than the other. Klara Jørgensen felt a sudden need to cry. A piece of chalk fell from the Professor's hand and turned to dust. Both turned their backs.

From then on Klara Jørgensen no longer gazed out of the window. Nor at her shoes. Nor at her hands. Nor at the book in front of her on the desk. It seemed to Gabriel Angélico that she didn't direct her gaze anywhere. It was as if she were blind or sleeping with her eyes open. As for him, he didn't dare look at her for fear she might meet his glance after all. Instead, he went rattling on between the rows of desks, a welter of conjunctions and adverbial clauses, propelled onward by the occasional ripple of laughter. If she hadn't said anything previously, she said even less now, and there was nothing Gabriel Angélico wanted more than to shut up. He'd never felt more of a clown than he did at this time. But silence was a luxury he couldn't afford. The space between the classroom's listening walls had continually to be filled the words, and it was his job to produce them.

Only towards her was he silent. Sometimes he thought she looked at him with an expectant air, as if she was yearning for a continuation of his clumsy revelations in the school courtyard.

But as soon as he believed he'd detected a glance from her quarter, her face would assume that vacuous mask again, and he would put the entire thing down to a mistaken fancy. He had decided never to approach her again. And so all he could do was carry on as before. These exhibitions cost him dear, and after the classes he would all but collapse behind his desk. He felt tired, like an exhausted winner and a beaten loser all at the same time. Everything was clear to him now, all the unnavigable troughs he must sail through and how they all led to her. But he was fearful that life hadn't equipped him for conquests like these. For her part, she continued to slip past him under the lemon trees, and he contemplated her naked shoulders and thought of how well they would sit under his hands if ever he dared to touch her. He looked at her ankles and wondered what it must be like to lay his own legs next to hers. What her palms would feel like against his cheeks. How this physical contact might possibly make her more real. But as yet she was just a miraculous illusion, like the cliffs on the coast he'd read about as a boy and tried to picture in his head.

Several days passed. He still came to the institute much too early in the morning and sat down to read the paper by the parrots' cage. Rosa Rama greeted him, the dean grunted as he passed, a sloshing cup of morning coffee in his hand, some of the students smiled to see the Professor sitting there. Then she would make her entrance, and the whole world would be filled with golden rays and frost at the same time. The words he was reading began to swim and his flesh puckered into goose pimples. Klara Jørgensen would be carrying her books the way she always did, against her breast like a wall of words, and would sit down on the bench at the other end of the

50

courtyard. There was an ocean between them. Her face was constantly hidden behind book covers. And so the tragi-comic charade went on, until one morning he noticed a tiny detail which all at once made her earthly again. She was sitting there reading his book. His name was printed on the first page and her index finger reached out and touched it like an invisible caress. She sat reading about his life. Suddenly he felt apprehensive and regretted giving her the work that contained so much about himself. He got up and walked straight across the courtyard until he was standing before her.

'You don't have to read that if you don't want,' he said rather sheepishly.

A fold appeared between her eyebrows and she looked up at him, without really meeting his gaze.

'Naturally I want to read it,' she replied. 'How else can I get to know you? You don't talk to me.'

His shoulders sagged and his hands fumbled in his trouser pockets. She gave a tiny smile. Then she lowered her eyes to the book again and the Professor stepped back and darted through the library door. Panting and motionless, he stood leaning up against a wall behind some stacks. He found it hard to believe that his body was designed for such shocks. In silence he closed his eyes and raised his left hand to his breast to deaden the sound of his wayward heart.

Gabriel Angélico's story was unlike anything Klara Jørgensen had read from that part of the world. The book was slim and succinct, it contained no flights of fancy or everyday miracles, no characters with spiritual gifts or inexplicable lineage. It wasn't typical of the powerful literature of Latin America, in which no natural or physical laws were allowed to apply. Gabriel Angélico's book was a simple story of a child who would disappear. It was his own story, about a little boy who had a tendency, constantly and unnoticed, to vanish, just as a shadow is swallowed by the sun or glides into an impenetrable gloom. Little Gabriel could sit motionless behind a rusty metal drum with his knees drawn up under his chin or hide in the cathedral vault by the side of a dead warrior. His hiding places were many, and he always found new ones. The only sad thing about the boy's repeated disappearing acts was that no one took the trouble to look for him. His mother explained this by saying that one rarely noticed Gabriel Angélico's taciturn presence. What he was thinking about behind that mask of silence was anyone's guess. Equally unfathomable was his face when, once again, he slid back into reality, after sitting on the veranda of a deserted house for three days without anyone wondering where he'd been.

His mother was a God-fearing woman. All the problems that had occurred at the time of the boy's baptism had been a sore trial to her. For four long years Gabriel Angélico had waited to be admitted into God's holy communion. Lightning had struck the Iglesia de la Santisima Trinidad the very night Ana Risueña started her contractions, and after that the church was under continual restoration. It was here that the family's newborn had always received the holy water, and there was no question of taking the boy all the way to the cathedral in the town centre to get him blessed. His grandmother, Florentina Alba, sweated blood to surround her grandson's cot with Jesus figures and prevent the Devil's wily hands from getting hold of him. Subsequently she wasn't certain that her labours had been rewarded, for the boy was as black as pitch and had the most seductive eyes anyone had ever seen in an infant. No christening was possible until enough money had been collected to rebuild the church steeple. So Ana Risueña found it advisable to name the child after an angel, and the boy was called Gabriel.

Little Gabriel Angélico had few, if any, friends. The chums he did have were of the sort that only he could see, and on the occasions he'd ventured to join in a game with his sister's dolls, his grandfather yanked him away by the ears saying that that sort of thing might turn his brain. Gabriel Angélico had never set eyes on his father. His father had just managed to make Gabriel's mother pregnant before dropping out of her life. After that, several other men had sought warmth in Ana Risueña's bed, but with no result apart from a little baby girl and a vestigial atmosphere of unrequited love within the house. From time to time his mother would worry that little Gabriel never seemed to talk to anyone, not even himself. But Florentina Alba said that was nothing to get upset about. When people are silent, said his grandmother, it's because they're talking to the angels. And from that day forth his family were certain that Gabriel Angélico went off occasionally to wander amongst the cherubim.

The first time Gabriel Angélico set foot inside a library, he thought the place was thoroughly magical. Its walls were lined with a knowledge that bore weightily down towards him, as he scraped his shoes against the smooth concrete floor. He stood before the shelves with open mouth, rather as other children experience their first meeting with a travelling circus. The certainty that everything he needed to know was gathered

53

in one place filled him with an all-pervasive serenity. As soon as he began primary school, Gabriel Angélico spent more time in the library than anywhere else, for the only book to be found in his own home was the Holy Scriptures. He had a good head, and at school he was always being moved up a class or two. Ana Risueña watched sceptically at the way the boy stole away to that evil book-pile instead of attending morning mass. In her opinion, so much knowledge all in one place could only lead to misery. By contrast, Florentina Alba was pleased the boy had found an interest, even though his sight soon began to deteriorate and no one knew where the money for glasses was going to come from. Each morning Florentina Alba prayed for help before the holy relics ingeniously arranged in an open kitchen cabinet. But when she got no answer, she snatched up a weeping version of the Virgen de Fatima and presented it to the optician's wife instead.

Gabriel Angélico had never set foot outside the mountains that enveloped him. He knew that the country he lived in was long and large and that the world beyond was even larger, but it had never occurred to him that he might travel himself. And so sometimes his innate restlessness troubled him to such an extent that he would sit and look at the mountains outside his window and fantasise about what lay beyond them. This was how he began to write. His own world seemed too dull to make a contribution to literature. Instead, by reading books, he learnt all about a world that wasn't his own. So Gabriel Angélico wrote one handwritten page after another about island kingdoms and ships, coral reefs and poppy fields, deserts and seas. He dreamt himself into these imaginary journeys of discovery so thoroughly that he soon began to believe he knew the world better than anyone else. When he finally got permission from his mother to climb the country's highest mountain and found himself at an altitude of 18,000 feet above sea level, he was certain he would see the ocean that everyone talked about. But the only thing Gabriel Angélico saw was mountains. There they were on every side, mightier and more complex than he'd ever seen them before. Beautiful, yes, but only mountains and nothing more. So, crestfallen, he descended from his illusory heights and began to write his *magnum opus* based on a world no larger than that encompassed by the mountain cleft he lived in.

Gabriel Angélico had always believed in God. In the beginning, he believed in the Almighty because he saw no reason not to. Everyday life was always full of incredible things, and even if most of Florentina Alba's prayers went unanswered, Gabriel Angélico could see how God continued to perform his miracles in the order that pleased him. Only when he discovered that his heart was in the wrong place did he realise that he was just such a miracle himself. On his first visit to the doctor he'd sat in a leather swivel chair, his feet not touching the ground, and listened as the good doctor told him how uncommon it was to be born with such a back-to-front body. In fact, it was little short of a miracle, the doctor told him. For a long time Gabriel Angélico pondered why God had done this thing and he was by no means convinced that his heart worked as it should. It was a doubt he'd never managed to shake off, either, but he comforted himself that if God had allowed him to function with a displaced heart, he ought, sometime, to be able to love with it too. For thirty long years Gabriel Angélico had waited for this to happen. The warmth and love he felt for his mother and sister came from quite different parts of his body, he thought, and still he hadn't felt the yearning the great romantics wrote about. But Gabriel Angélico was a patient man. He believed in fate, in the idea that two people are made for one another and that the one would never be fulfilled without the other. And so it had to be for him as well. He hadn't been born under a lucky star. On the contrary, he'd come into the world accompanied by a flash of lightning. And for thirty years he'd waited for love to strike him with the same prodigious force.

Klara Jørgensen stood before Gabriel Angélico's house by the river, one leg twined around the other. She stood some yards away and stared at the lop-sided building which had hunched itself against the frowning mountains poised above it. Plaster was peeling from the walls and the roof was about to give way beneath the branches of an olive tree. The door was open, but there was nothing to be seen within. The sun cast its shadows in all directions. She stood like this for perhaps half an hour, until her hands were clammy with apprehension, and her legs ached. She budged not an inch, although it took an age before Gabriel Angélico came out on to the steps and saw her standing there. She seemed almost invisible in all the afternoon dust, and Gabriel Angélico mused to himself that this was what spirits must look like. For one brief moment they stood gazing at each other. Then Gabriel Angélico pushed his hands into his pockets and went out to meet her.

He stood before her and she held out the book to him without a word. He took it in his slim hands and put it under his arm. Klara Jørgensen rubbed the tip of one shoe against her leg and looked down. Gabriel Angélico didn't know where to turn his eyes. He wanted to say something beautiful, about eternity and the love of one human being for another, about fate and the insanity of life.

'Would you like something to drink?' he asked instead.

She cast an enquiring glance at the twisted chairs in the shade of the olive tree.

'Yes, perhaps,' she said.

Gabriel Angélico couldn't tell whether this meant yes or no, so he waited until she started to walk towards the house. Then he began to follow her. Without another word she took her place in one of the braided chairs in front of the steps and stretched her legs carefully out in front of her.

'What would you like?' he asked.

'Lemonade,' she answered.

He nodded wordlessly, his arms hanging limp. Then he went in to his mother, who was in the kitchen performing her customary poundings on some strong maize dough. What had he been thinking of? In reality he had nothing to offer, there wasn't a lemon to be found in the kitchen, not even an orange or a passion fruit.

'Have we got any lemonade?' Gabriel Angélico whispered to his mother.

'What do you want that for?' Ana Risueña enquired without lifting her eyes from the dough.

'For drinking,' he replied.

His mother glanced up, her hands made deformed and clumpy by the moist dough.

'You want lemonade now?'

'I've had lemonade before,' he said.

'You've never drunk lemonade these thirty years,' said his mother.

Ana Risueña shook her head so that her entire breast rocked from side to side.

'Have you got a visitor?'

Gabriel Angélico began to perspire.

'I've got to have lemonade,' was all he said.

'Then go and pick yourself some lemons,' said his mother, turning back to her work.

Gabriel Angélico rushed out of the back door, across the parched grass to the grey brick house at the end of the yard. The house belonged to La Niña and her mother, and was little more than four brick walls and a staircase that led up to a first floor that had never been completed. A black labrador with a dusty coat and a gammy leg chased cockroaches round the floor. La Niña was in the kitchen with the ornaments she hawked from door to door spread out on a piece of thick paper. She was a beautiful girl, who had no need to prostitute herself to get money out of men. It was enough that she visited them in their living-rooms and told them a bit about the jewellery she travelled around with. As a rule she'd get a little money, even though she left nothing behind her.

'Is it all right if I pick some lemons?' Gabriel Angélico asked with no further explanation.

'Pick away,' answered La Niña, without removing her gaze from the tarnished baubles.

Gabriel Angélico nodded and went out into the yard again. The lemon tree stood halfway between the two houses, practically entwined with a smaller one, a nutmeg tree. The nutmeg tree had been the object of considerable discussion

58

over the years between Victor Alba and La Niña's grandfather, Carlos Pellegrini, because nutmeg was known to be a delectable spice. Victor Alba had chained himself to the tree on repeated occasions, with the idea of demonstrating that it was his, while Carlos Pellegrini produced his land title and a tape measure in support of his claim. It was a meaningless discussion and wholly academic, for neither of the two men could abide the taste of nutmeg. Even so, the notion of sharing the tree was out of the question as all their petty squabbling had caused a mutual bitterness. Instead, Carlos Pellegrini put up a fence where he believed the boundary ran and incorporated both the lemons and the nutmegs into his garden. He barred the gate with a great wooden beam and that was the last time Victor Alba set foot in his neighbour's house while old Pellegrini lived. La Niña's grandfather had long since died, the fence had been taken down and no one gave either the lemons or the nutmegs a second thought. But Gabriel Angélico thought it best to ask before picking any, well aware that the seeds of animosity grew fast in that continent's scorched earth.

Klara Jørgensen sat with her eyes closed and one hand on the back of her neck. She hadn't heard him come. Gabriel Angélico stood in the doorway with his mouth agape, while the little ripples in the jug threatened to spill the lemonade. The sun rained sparks at the girl who sat there in front of him. She was so near that his heart was leaping out of his breast and he had to clench his fist over it to keep it in place. He could see the skin on her arm breathing, the slight membrane of dampness that covered it in the sultry heat, pimples and

59

birthmarks, the delicate, angular elbow. She had her hair drawn back into a pony-tail, and he stole a secret glance at her neck, at the artery that throbbed and the wisps of hair that had escaped from the knot. He saw the hand that rested on her neck, the beginning of her jawbone and the wrinkles that appeared on her throat when she tilted her head slightly. She was so close, but it was more than Gabriel Angélico's life was worth to touch her. She was sacred and unique in his world and, like a valued museum piece, could only be contemplated from afar. It was as if the slightest touch on his part would cause their two worlds to shatter.

He poured lemonade into the two glasses and placed the jug on the loose flagstone by the door. She turned to him and smiled as he held out the glass to her. He sat down, unable to speak for a while after she'd bestowed such a smile on him. Instead, he leant back and tried to get used to the thought that she was there, in jeans and trainers, outside his house, inside his world, deep in the hollow palm of the mountains. She, who had always been so far away from him, sat there now drinking lemonade in small sips, her lips barely touching the rim of the glass. She sat next to him, as if she'd always occupied that chair, under that bough, holding that glass loosely in her hand. And Gabriel Angélico wondered if he'd ever be able to view such a scene as commonplace, rather than the miracle he now felt it was.

They were silent for a long time. She contemplated the mountains as if there was something thrilling about them, something he was incapable of seeing. He'd long since ceased noticing those heaps of stone whose outline he blotted out each evening when he dowsed the light.

'Do you still write books?' she asked at last.

'No,' he replied.

'Why not?'

'I can't do it properly.'

'Have you written many before?'

'Yes. But most of them are handwritten and in a drawer.'

'What are they about?' she asked.

'Everything I know nothing of.'

'Ah.'

'Yes, apart from the one you've read. That's about me.'

She smiled softly and brushed a fly from her leg.

'Are your stories sad?'

'Mostly,' answered the Professor.

'I think that's good.'

'Oh?'

'Yes.'

There was something calm about her voice now, as if his nearness no longer frightened her.

'I don't think there's anything like the really great sorrows,' she said.

The Professor nodded.

'Only the tragic is genuinely beautiful, because it never gets the chance to be trivial,' she went on. 'When two people find each other, they suddenly become so pathetically commonplace. They become people like our fathers and mothers, they forget love's finer points and start to believe in convention instead.'

She spoke the words slowly in Spanish with just a hint of a foreign accent.

'Tragedies are beautiful. People love and then they die. And that's that.'

Gabriel Angélico was suddenly seized with sadness at her words.

'It might have been better if they'd been allowed to go on living,' he said.

'Why?' she said. 'They're only in books. They're not real.'

He said nothing.

'You don't seriously believe, Professor, that any modern human being would die for the sake of love.'

'I don't know,' he said.

'Never in a million years,' she said.

Then she drank the last dregs from her glass and looked up at him with the eyes of a child.

'May I have another?'

With trembling hands Gabriel Angélico crushed ice and squeezed lemons. He was happy, but overcome and befuddled by her proximity. He was in a dream now. The bitter aftertaste would come later, and he would go to sleep in the knowledge that he would lie there alone for the rest of his life. The day would almost certainly come when he would hate these mountains, this view, the waterfalls that sang and the empty chair that would sigh for her long after she was gone.

She was still staring at the mountains. Gabriel Angélico handed her a fresh glass of lemonade and seated himself beside her once again. He sighed at the wooded slopes before them and took a long draught that gurgled in his chest.

'I used to dream about what was behind them,' he said, as if he was talking to himself in his sleep. 'But there's nothing but mountains. That's all there is.'

'Nonsense,' she said. 'There are jungles and plains and seas as well. Haven't you seen them?'

'No.'

'You should travel more, Professor.'

'Maybe. It takes an eternity to get down from here.'

'Not at all. You could fly across the Andes and be on the coast before dark.'

'That isn't for me,' he replied quite simply.

He knew she wouldn't understand that for him to buy a one-way ticket would mean starving his family and working himself to death. Klara Jørgensen simply nodded and drew the conclusion that he was frightened of flying.

'I've often wondered what the sea looks like,' he said.

'The sea,' she repeated with tranquillity in her voice.

'Once I climbed up into the mountains to see it, but it was out of sight.'

'The sea is unpredictable,' she said. 'It can swallow a person in its ruthlessness.'

'I don't fear it,' said the Professor.

'No? You can drown as easily as anyone else.'

'I would never go where it was deep.'

'Because you're scared?'

'Because I can't swim.'

'That surprises me, Professor. You can do so many things.'

'I've never needed to swim, so I can't.'

'What do you want with the sea, then?'

'To sit still and listen to the sound of it.'

He turned to her and smiled, and then the strangest thing

63

happened. She looked, not past him, but directly into his face. And she smiled back, with a look that was quite unafraid. His hands went clammy and his lips numb and his heart twisted about inside him with little pangs of pain.

The sun faded and she sat up. There was something reluctant about her movements, although the rickety chair could hardly have been comfortable for her. He would have sat there all night with her if she'd wanted. He could have watched her sleeping until the sun rose, though birds might have defecated on him and spiders nipped his skin.

'I'll have to go now,' she said, sighing at the final dregs of the sunset.

'Yes,' said Gabriel Angélico.

'I could stay here forever,' she said.

'Then stay,' he said.

She turned towards him and studied him for a moment, her face full of earnestness. Then she turned up her mouth in a smile and replied:

'Well, obviously I couldn't do that.'

'No, obviously,' said Gabriel Angélico.

'One day I'll have forgotten all this,' she said.

There were traces of relief in her face.

'I'm in a waking dream. Soon it will pass.'

Gabriel Angélico clutched his breast and tried to conceal the fact that she'd just wounded him. Klara Jørgensen rose with a small bound and eased her legs. She stretched her arms and smiled at him. She no longer seemed nervous about anything now – quite the opposite. It looked as if she'd gone through the same movements hundreds of times.

'So long, Professor,' she said lightly.

'So long, Miss Klara,' he said.

She turned away and left him.

Gabriel Angélico sat watching her outline as it disappeared into the darkness of the riverbank. Only then did it occur to him that not a single person had passed by and seen them sitting there. Not even a stray cat or an unfaithful husband had slunk by. It had been just him and her and the olive tree, and Gabriel Angélico knew that he wouldn't sleep that night. Her visit had been just a brief intermezzo in an endless round of predictable days. It hadn't made her more mortal, just confirmed him in the belief that it was the idea of her he'd been clinging to all his life. The sight of the empty chair brought a bitter taste to his mouth. The seat was still half depressed, as if waiting for her return. He knew that he would wait too, just as he'd waited for thirty years in the knowledge that when she finally turned up, he would recognise her immediately. So it had been. And from that day on his world would always be tinged by her presence, or the lack of it.

Klara Jørgensen disembarked from a charter flight on to the Venezuelan island of Vidabella, with her mouth open, like some stranded fish the tide has forgotten. It was the girl's first meeting with Latin America. The Caribbean air was thick and heavy, like some foul dying breath, and dripping with humidity, whereas the ground beneath it was barren and as dry as tinder. The trees stood like misshapen growth before her and writhed in pain in their craving for water. The sand seemed to be waiting for a gust of wind that might carry it to a place where it could, eventually, feel the touch of water. From the air the island had looked small and wasted, surrounded by a moribund coral reef which made it look like an ashen jellyfish in the sea. From the ground it looked smaller still and the landscape seemed to contract even more in the equatorial sun. It had been six months since the last rain had fallen on Vidabella and the most recent shower, around Easter, hadn't managed to penetrate the soil's crust properly.

Vidabella was so small that a drive from one side to the other would take less than an hour. Four small settlements were dotted around its coast. Puerto de las Naves was the biggest with discotheques, shopping avenues and hotels, as well as strip-clubs for the randy men who holidayed alone. The road westwards led over high cliffs that plunged inexorably down to the mouth of a bay and quiet Santa Ana. There was only one hotel in this small fishing town and a clutch of restaurants. One establishment was owned by Don Pepe Paraiso, a powerfully built Italian who had taught the islanders how to bake pizzas in brick ovens. The restaurant was adjacent to the largest coco-palm on the beach and had a pleasant terrace where one could sip fruit punch beneath white canvas parasols and see the fishermen come in out of the sunset like black silhouettes. A stone's throw away was La Naranja, a small place with funeral-grey tableclothes and a rough cement floor. Here the manager could be seen spending lonely evenings smoking non-stop, his hand faithfully clutching a glass of whisky, as he stared at some lopsidedness in its décor. As a rule he contented himself by sighing over it and taking it as an omen that the time had come to put the cork back in the bottle.

Hesitantly, Klara Jørgensen pushed open the door of the little beach house which from that day on was to be her home. It was as if the very air inside it stretched out transparent fingers and embraced her. The floor was of rough-hewn timber, the walls were covered with bamboo and the windows hadn't been washed for a good while. A long wooden breakfast-bar separated the kitchen from the living-room and on the end of it stood a basket of fruit the ripeness of which could already be smelt. The living-room was furnished with an uncomfortable wooden sofa and a bookcase whose empty shelves gaped silently at her. Beneath the window in the middle of the room was a writing desk. It looked new and seemed overcome by this realm of shadows and dust.

'For you,' said William Penn. 'So you'll be able to study.'

She smiled and turned to the Captain who stood behind her. For several weeks he'd been awaiting her arrival. Now she was standing there examining the desk he'd given her, before she carried her suitcase to the bedroom. From the doorway she stood looking at the huge double bed made of painted wood.

'Do I sleep here?' she asked.

He looked at her.

'Unless you prefer the hammock.'

She smiled cautiously and glanced through the front door at the hammock which rocked in the breeze on the patio.

'It's the biggest bed I've ever seen,' she said.

Slowly she approached it.

'Which side is mine?'

He shrugged.

'Whichever you like.'

She sat on the edge of the bed and ran the palm of her hand over the bedspread. Her eyes wandered back and forth from one side to the other. He went over to her and crouched down at her feet.

'Will you like it here?' he asked.

'Yes, why shouldn't I?'

'And what do you think of the place?'

'It's a place like any other.'

'Yes, that's true.'

Suddenly she got the urge to start unpacking. The Captain watched her from the bed as she enthusiastically sorted drawers and cupboards, as if establishing herself in a strange room gave her a kind of pleasure. For an instant she reminded him of a little girl playing at houses with her friends, and the enthusiasm

68

in her eyes flew straight across the room and settled like a warm ember in his heart.

Klara Jørgensen arrived in Vidabella with fifteen novels and a Spanish word list. It was three days before she ventured out alone. She found the little town unappealing and half-dead at first, and she had to point out even the smallest item to the shopkeepers in lieu of the right words. The gabble of voices on the pavement was unintelligible to her and for weeks she didn't speak to a soul. If she couldn't find what she was looking for on the supermarket shelves, she chose something else rather than seek help, and she never asked for directions if she got lost. The townspeople glanced inquisitively at her as she wandered about with a pink shopping net and her excessively warm clothes, which she gradually replaced with cool dresses and loose skirts. To begin with she looked pale and almost ill, but soon she was the same golden colour as the tourists from Florida and her brown hair bleached a little and made her eyes seem larger in her face. No one really knew where she came from or what she was doing on the island, but it seemed she never tired of books.

Santa Ana was a dirty, but pleasant little town. Klara Jørgensen arrived when the *gallito* trees were still blooming in all their blushing beauty and Caribbean winds swathed sweaty faces in the morning heat. In addition to the small hotel and the restaurants on the beach, the town had a Chinese eatery that was run by three generations of a twelve-strong family from Beijing. Close by was a tumbledown casino, a ludicrous copy of the Taj Mahal, which had been closed since the change of governors. The most frequented corner of the place was

Rafael el Grande's liquor store, and Sunday was the big day for drinking. Then, workers and officials, fishermen and shopkeepers would go straight from morning mass to drown their prayers in rum and cola. Even the church was semi-delapidated and lay there sighing at the memory of its former glory, though it was still filled to bursting each Sunday with a welter of fans, crossings and agonised song. Behind the church lay the town's own Plaza Bolívar, with its wind-blown trash and its whitewashed tree-trunks that prevented pests from gaining a foothold unobserved. The obligatory bust of the country's liberator even had its hairline picked out in bird droppings, like some shameful caste mark on the general's proud forehead.

Next to the beach was the greengrocer's small premises from which the smell of over-ripe bananas wafted out into the street. The Arabs' shops were terraced along the promenade and sold fringed bathing towels and Colombian underwear, and anything else they could pick up on their business trips to Panama. Down on the shore was the blue-painted police office in which the chief superintendent dozed behind a massive desk while the figure of Jesus Christ glanced down at him from a lonely crucifix on the wall. The children played football under dim lights in the park while their mothers gave suck to infants. The fishing boats returned from the sea, sailed by burnished men with skins tanned by the sun who stood at the helm of their boats, some large, some small, each bearing the name of the woman they had loved and lost, painted in silent testament on the bow.

In the mornings Klara Jørgensen walked to the market on the little prominence above the town. At first she'd thought it a bedlam of cackling hens, chickens who bravely went to their deaths on the wet cement floor, and women who cried out their sons' catches, until it all sounded like some ghastly echo in the reverberating hall. For the first few days she just stood there and stared at glistening kidneys laid out on crooked counters, gaping fish with fever-red gills, entrails that hung down from the roof and a slaughtered ox that still hadn't stopped bleeding. At first, standing by the door, she had seemed like a small, frightened animal herself, but after a while all the impressions sifted into her consciousness and settled there. Subsequently, they became a part of daily life, just as all curiosities and unfamiliar elements eventually melt into the backdrop of the mundane, until one can't ever remember viewing them as the least bit peculiar.

She tried gradually to accustom herself to the thought of being a half of something. She could linger in the bedroom doorway, still bemused by the formal, wide bed which she now shared with a man. His bedside table sported a packet of cigarettes, a couple of Mexican comics and endless piles of receipts that he never got round to sorting. Her side was overflowing with notes, a compendium and at least three novels she would probably read within the week. On hot days, when the temperature in the living-room was unbearable, she would sit in bed and write with books strewn all over the counterpane. Sometimes the Captain would come in, his hands covered with oil after doing some repair job on the car, and see her sitting there, smiling apologetically amidst all her mess.

'I'm fond of reading,' she'd say.

'And I'm fond of tinkering,' he'd reply.

Klara Jørgensen was good at grammatical analyses and

composing perfect essays on all the many literary techniques. But she couldn't cook. Klara Jørgensen knew only too well that William Penn wasn't worried about Ibsen's retrospective technique, although as a rule he'd listen with interest because he realised she had no one else to talk to. But what the Captain needed when he got home was a meal that could be heated up quickly while he rinsed off the sea salt with water from the grey plastic tank. Klara Jørgensen knew nothing about filleting or seasoning. She feared frying times and oven temperatures far more than the hungry look on the Captain's face. But, after serving him an impressive array of variations on the sandwich, Klara Jørgensen decided she had to invest in some cookery books. Spanish culinary jargon, combined with her general ignorance of domestic economy, produced the most original results. Finally, Klara Jørgensen decided to swallow her fear of strangers and seek out the islander she regarded as the least intimidating.

Klara Jørgensen discovered the old man in the Chinese eatery. Ernest Reiser sat hunched over a steaming wun tun soup, eating with bony fingers and with the waitress, Yin Li, opposite him. There was no conversation because Yin Li had sufficient Spanish only to take food orders. The décor was of lavish, red velour, with plush walls and two Chinese lanterns, only one of which was working. On the long bar counter sat a heavy, ancient television set that was never switched off. Occasionally the old man would rest his spoon and nod brusquely at the screen.

'Anyone dead?'
'No yet.'

'Well, switch over then.'

Klara Jørgensen stood amongst the myriad of wooden beads that hung in the doorway and looked around with uncertainty in her face. Apart from Ernest Reiser and the girl, the room was empty except for the usual alley cats which were allowed in on sufferance to catch a cockroach or two. In an attempt to be noticed, Klara Jørgensen gave a little cough and Ernest Reiser lifted his head to look her way.

'Well, it's our young lady, isn't it?' was all he said and went on slurping his soup.

Klara Jørgensen rubbed her hands tentatively and slowly approached.

'Sit down,' he said, nodding and without taking his eyes from the television screen. 'What can I do for you?'

Already she regretted coming, but she could hardly turn back now that she'd revealed herself.

'I can't cook,' she said.

'Well,' said the old man.

He pushed away the soup bowl, which had been scraped clean.

'Is that anything to get worried about?'

'The Captain is hungry in the evenings.'

'And you plan to cook for him?'

'Yes.'

'How old are you, Miss Klara?'

'Twenty-one.'

'Is this your first trip to the Caribbean?'

'Yes.'

'And you're here because of him?'

'Yes.'

73

'And now you want to cook.'

'Yes.'

Ernest Reiser's gaze wandered out through the wooden beads in the doorway and he half shook his head.

'Oh, amorous liaisons, amorous liaisons,' he mumbled. 'They make us do the oddest things. Send us to the oddest places.'

'Sorry?' she said.

'Nothing, my dear,' he said. 'Tell me, do you know how to watch the time?'

'Yes.'

'Then you can cook.'

She looked at him with a degree of amazement.

'Come along,' said Ernest Reiser, and he rose, his belt buckle jingling. 'Let's make the Captain a bean soup.'

'How?' she asked.

'What do we need?' the old man asked, lighting a cigarette butt that had been secreted in his trouser pocket.

'Beans?'

'Good. What else?'

She looked completely at a loss.

'I don't know.'

'Tomatoes, my dear, and fresh coriander if we can get it.'

Then he brushed a speck of ash from his thigh and began to make for the exit. Klara Jørgensen gave the television a quick glance and registered that two men in Caracas had killed each other over three cold beers in a fridge. With a slight shrug of her shoulders she turned to follow the old man.

From that day forth Klara Jørgensen spent each afternoon with

Ernest Reiser in the restaurant kitchen. There were no diners so early in the evening, and she'd gradually got bored spending her days reading. The fifteen novels she'd brought with her had long since been read, and now she was struggling through contemporary South American authors in their mother tongue. Ernest Reiser taught her how to cut up fish, batter chicken and make an excellent pasta sauce, and occasionally he'd help her with some Spanish idiom. He taught her the names of every kind of fruit and herb in the shops, showed her how to make corn-cakes and shred meat the Venezuelan way, how to cook beans and which bananas were best for frying. And he laughed at the fact that he was so used to the kitchen himself, explaining it away by saying that he'd always been a bachelor at heart, but had once allowed himself to be beguiled by a frenetic love affair. He smiled as he said it, but Klara Jørgensen thought she could detect traces of pain in his eyes, as he turned his head back to the steaming stove.

Perhaps there was more relief than joy to be spied in the Captain's face when at last Klara Jørgensen began to serve him up an evening meal every day. He enjoyed what was put in front of him, at least that was what he said, and she chose to take him at his word as she did in most things. Her grandiose dinner plans were only sporadically frustrated by the water shortage. It was the worst in the island's history and had lasted almost two years. The submarine pipe that carried water to the island from the mainland had become completely blocked, and instead the ferry arrived each Monday bearing great lorries full of water that had to be rationed out by the local water company. Everyone had half an hour of mains water in the morning and in the evening, and that was all. In the beginning people had protested by setting fire to car tyres in the streets, but gradually rationing had become a way of life. Some clearly profited from this sorry state of affairs, like the island's governor, who'd made good money from the grey plastic tanks he manufactured.

Klara Jørgensen survived her early days on Vidabella out of pure curiosity. Later listlessness set in, and so did the desire for things that could not be had. She yearned periodically for the security of home and the television programmes, autumn evenings and trams, the library's cosy evening light. Sometimes she missed the cold – well, not the cold itself, perhaps, but coming in from it, from attacking chilly gusts, to huddle beneath a blanket and feel the warmth caressing her body. Not heavy and sticky like tropical nights in the Caribbean, but subdued and sensuous like an embrace. She missed the way a mouthful of red wine could thaw her out on a frosty-edged winter day and the feeling of the ice-cold bathroom floor beneath her feet in the mornings. She hankered for those prayers that summer might last for ever, and the knowledge that it never would. She longed for streets covered with leaves, cathedral bells in the October afternoon sun and the Christmas displays in Oslo's department stores. Without seasons the world seemed changeless and uneventful all at once, nothing altered or burst upon the scene, each morning she awoke to the same merciless heat and sun, always sun.

That Christmas was to be the saddest of Klara Jørgensen's life. They celebrated it at the restaurant by the beach, with Ernest Reiser, Carmen de la Cruz, Henrik Branden, Bianca Lizardi and the barman, Umberto. Nothing was like it was at home. The Father Christmases looked pathetic in front of the shrivelled bushes, and an over-large Christmas tree towered above the bar, weighed down with tinsel and tasteless decoration. Henrik Branden had employed the breakfast cook from Santa Ana's only hotel to prepare the food, a task that was strictly beyond his culinary competence and natural talent. The result was a menu of ham and omelette, together with the driest turkey ever eaten in those latitudes. Klara Jørgensen longed for brandy-snaps. She tried to conjure them up in her memory, golden and crunchy. But instead of contributing a comment about the Christmas cakes of home, Klara Jørgensen poured herself a brandy for each sad thought that came into her head. She didn't usually get drunk like this, but it was Christmas Eve, she was far from home and she drank heavily without anyone seeming to notice.

She always felt loneliest in the company of others. Klara Jørgensen didn't have the Captain's ability to adjust to the company in which she found herself, nor any talent at preventing conversations from petering out. She found Bianca Lizardi particularly difficult to communicate with, because the waitress seldom had the time to let Klara Jørgensen get her tongue round her Spanish phrases. Ernest Reiser poured himself one whisky after another with the dexterity of a sleep-walker. Now and then his sarcasm would flow across the table, only to fizzle out above the food, which had gradually been appropriated by the flies. Carmen de la Cruz seemed to have succeeded in entertaining both the Captain and her man, and was doing quite a bit of guffawing herself, rasping up her throat with all her cackling. Bianca Lizardi sent her ugly glances, while Klara Jørgensen's pupils showed like two warning lamps. After a while Umberto got up and began to clear the table. Bianca Lizardi followed him. A moment later there was a scream.

That evening Bianca Lizardi had become innocently embroiled in an argument between Umberto the barman and the breakfast cook over the remains of the macabre turkey. The cook had grabbed the meat cleaver in order to threaten Umberto, and Bianca Lizardi had got in the way of an aggressive lunge and had had her hand sliced. White in the face, the young woman sat down and looked at the blood that was welling up from the gaping wound between her thumb and the rest of her hand. It formed a little pool on the dirty floor between her feet and, if it did nothing else, the sight of blood quickly made the two men forget their disagreement. A moment later Henrik Branden burst in and rushed a napkin to Bianca Lizardi, followed by several more. Bianca Lizardi sat as if paralysed, while Henrik Branden detailed Carmen de la Cruz to drive her to the hospital, as she was the one who'd had the least to drink. Neither woman looked particularly happy about the arrangement, but they left at once. Bianca Lizardi was silent and pale as she clutched the material packed round her hand, certain that her thumb would fall off at any moment.

'How are you feeling?' asked Carmen de la Cruz with a Belmont hanging from the corner of her mouth.

'If I don't die from losing a thumb, I might from the way you're driving this car,' said a tight-lipped Bianca Lizardi.

'Take it easy,' replied Carmen, who knew better than to let such comments get to her. 'Did you know that I once worked as a policewoman in Caracas?'

'Really. Isn't this what they do to thieves in countries where they have the Koran?' said Bianca Lizardi, seemingly unaffected and with a glance at her thumb. A deep quiver of her lower lip gave her away. She was in agony.

'But you haven't stolen anything, have you?'

'No. It's life that's the greatest thief.'

Carmen de la Cruz wound up the window and switched on the air conditioning.

'Go ahead and bawl if you like.'

But Bianca Lizardi had never bawled in her life, and wasn't about to begin now.

'Just drive,' she said.

Sewing the thumb securely back on to Bianca Lizardi's hand cost a million bolívars. The bill was paid by Henrik Branden with a liberal cheque to the hospital's director, who himself had an artificial eye. The thumb would always be useless, but at least it was there and, provided she didn't try to lift more than two plates at once, no one would notice that it had almost landed on the surgeon's floor. Bianca Lizardi had to remain in hospital overnight and Carmen de la Cruz did too, though she insisted the doctors said nothing to the patient about her sitting there waiting. Instead she talked to her other half who had come to sign the cheque, and who commented on how strange it was that Bianca Lizardi appeared to be without either relatives or friends on the island.

'There's nothing strange about it,' replied Carmen de la Cruz. 'Bianca has inflated ideas about romance. That's how one ends up alone.'

Klara Jørgensen was left on the beach with the Captain and

Ernest Reiser. She thought the three of them made a sorry sight: old Ernest half asleep in his uncomfortable plastic chair, the Captain smoking continuously and much more than usual, and she herself, who had got through half a bottle of brandy on her own without saying a word. William Penn glanced at her as she sat glassy-eyed, wringing her hands mechanically, as if she were about to lose her wits.

'Klara? Aren't you feeling too good?'

Klara Jørgensen shook her head slowly just as the moisture in her eyes was on the point of overflowing. She tried to stand up, but stumbled at once, lurching sideways into the table. The Captain rose calmly and shook Ernest Reiser to tell the old man that it might be sensible to turn in. Then the Captain took Klara Jørgensen by the hand and they walked down the beach. She looked at the lights from the beach house with a doll-like gaze. After a while she asked the Captain to stop. William Penn had drunk enough in his life to know that even the shortest stroll could seem insuperable in such a state. Klara Jørgensen knelt down at the water's edge, threw up twice and began to sob. William Penn put his arms around her and said nothing, but in the silence of that moment he felt he'd failed in something he'd long since determined to do. The waves came in, like soft palms patting their feet. Klara Jørgensen hadn't even taken her shoes off. She had stones in them. The street lights went out and the moon contented itself by casting a turbid gleam on the water.

'Do you want to go home, Klara?' William Penn asked, clasping her face between his hands. 'Can't you take any more?'

She wiped the salt from her face with a corner of her sleeve. 'I'm tired. I want to go home,' she said.

'I understand. On the first plane. I promise.'

A little furrow formed in Klara Jørgensen's face. She looked uncomprehendingly at the Captain for a moment.

'I want to go home,' she said. 'There's nowhere I need to fly to.'

She pulled off both her shoes and carried them in her hands, as she began to walk barefoot across the sand.

The feeling of being at home in the Caribbean did eventually settle on Klara Jørgensen. It came flowing like a sea-current, unnoticed and unseen. After a while she took the days as they came. There was something accustomed and tedious about them, but also something secure and welcoming. Gradually she ceased to be frightened, too. Frightened she might use the wrong words, ask the most banal questions, take root there or have made the wrong choice in ever coming at all. The feeling of having chosen the right island and the right Captain was never wholly there. Or rather, it came the way it commonly does between two people who get to know each other under the exceptional conditions represented by sleeping in the same bed, eating from the same fridge, showering under the same rose and sharing the same piece of time in what is a human life. Thus, she ceased to fear William Penn too, but could ask him to brush his teeth and wash his feet without it causing her embarrassment, share the bathroom with him in the mornings, walk about naked from room to room, smile at her collapsed apple pie and laugh out loud if she should happen to thump him in her sleep. The drama of those first days died away and was replaced by a deep peace, sealed with light, familiar kisses, a caressed stomach, closeness without words or gestures. Two bodies next to each other in a wide bed, tied up together at a mooring, anchored not merely on common ground or passion, but on love's humdrum acoustic.

Of all his seventeen grandchildren, Gabriel Angélico was the one Victor Alba felt least affection for. When he was small the boy had come bearing bunches of flowers like some kind of hippie and his grandfather remarked dryly that his mother ought to put him in a skirt. His eyes glistened like two puddles in the sun and he was so delicate that the draught from the living-room window could bowl him over. He never played matador with the mechanic's black labrador or asked to be allowed to tighten up the valves on some old jeep in the workshop. The only times he had grazes on his knees were when the other children forced him to the ground and beat him up because they were bored. As an adult, however, Gabriel Angélico had become much more personable, walking at his full height down streets and alleys, in steady procession with himself. Victor Alba knew all about his grandson's popularity with his students, but didn't alter his opinion on that account. All he could see was Gabriel Angélico's delicate soul, his soft chracter and his lack of those attributes which, taken together, make up a man.

Victor Alba shuddered at the sight of his grandson's thin belly, the subcutaneous fat that lay in thin folds, his lanky legs and restrained face. His hands, though, were what the grandfather found most repugnant, those fragile paws that leafed elegantly through reference works and anthologies, or held a pen lightly as he wrote and which never became sore no matter how near, mentally, he wrote himself to death. Hands like those couldn't work. They bore witness to nothing whatever in the shape of skill or experience, they were merely smooth and unused, like a pair of new kid gloves. Useless to everyone, unable to protect, support or kindle desire in a woman's body. Victor Alba had long since accepted that his grandson would never marry. Nor did he entertain any hope that he might notch himself up the requisite number of mistresses required to maintain a respectable bachelor existence. There was so little allure about his grandson's slight figure that Victor Alba couldn't understand why a total stranger of a girl began to appear in the evenings outside the house by the river. She always came the same way and always sat in the same chair, in the same position, just to be by Gabriel Angélico's side until the sun melted away.

Gabriel Angélico trusted to fate. So he wasn't all that surprised by Klara Jørgensen's appearances. The evening after her very first visit she returned. He saw her by the river's edge where he'd seen her previously, standing irresolute, peering at the house and not knowing whether to back away or step forward. Once again he stood looking at her for a brief moment, as he searched for her gaze in the myriad of motes, and imagined that with this wall of dust between them he could permit himself to look into her eyes. Only when he began to feel symptoms of asthma, did he take a step in her direction. She saw it and came to meet him. Again they stood facing each other with evasive glances, anxious about the intimacy these meetings produced. He could have reached out a hand and touched her if it hadn't been for his conviction that such an approach would ruin everything.

'Are you thirsty?' he asked, as he had before.

'Yes,' she answered.

And she gave a hazy smile and then went to sit down beneath the crooked boughs of the olive tree.

Gabriel Angélico wondered what a girl like her did when she wasn't sitting by his side. Did she consume mouth-watering cakes with her friends in the town's cafés? Or drink bittersweet coffee at the baker's counter? Did she queue at the ticket window of the cinema with some male student? Or sit alone on a bench outside the cathedral in deep concentration over her reading? Did she lie in one of those front gardens where the streets were wreathed in rose hedges and gilded post-boxes? It struck him that he knew nothing whatever about her life, or how she normally filled her days. But this didn't seem to mean all that much to her. Not now, now that she chose instead to sit with him for hour after hour, for eternities filled with silence and simple presence. Day after day she returned, but she never knocked or advertised her arrival in any way. She simply waited by the water until she saw him in the doorway, and he always made sure to look out for her at the same hour. After a few weeks he didn't even have to go to her, he just sat there and waited for her to glide down into the chair next to him. So, imperceptibly, evening after evening, she drank in his world, during this interlude that had become his time of grace.

Gabriel Angélico had never had visits from a girl before. The family peeped with concealed curiosity at the small figure from behind the faded lace curtains of the living-room window. As soon as she came, they retreated from the steps and left the chairs empty, to follow events clandestinely from the tasselled velvet sofas of the oven-like sitting-room. No one could hear what the two of them said out there, because their voices were low and were easily drowned by the constant whirring of the fans on the ceiling. Often they said nothing at all, just sat quietly with their hands in their laps, breathing imperceptibly. Neither his mother nor his sister dared ask Gabriel Angélico where the girl came from and he never referred to her after she'd left. Nor did they know what sort of relationship he had with her, but his restlessness at the dinner table and his repeated glances out of the window indicated that it was serious. At the same time, his mother noticed how the pile of handwritten manuscript on his work-table ceased to grow, that her son seemed not to be writing any more, but instead sat staring out at the mountains after the girl had gone. Gabriel Angélico stopped writing anything at all, stopped eating supper and breakfast, stopped smiling at dinner-time or reading poetry. Everything, apart from waiting, gazing through colourless curtains and shutters, to see if she were coming.

Initially she was reserved and spoke little. Gabriel Angélico didn't burden her with chat or try to charm her in any way. His words were subdued and serious, as if he was stealing cautiously along the paths of her consciousness. Sometimes he would ask her about the world and get ideas in return, images of the streets of Rome, the eating houses of London, the blue light of the Aegean and the scrawny trees of the south of France. She had been everywhere and knew about everything that was squalid and moving, abhorrent and thrilling in this small world.

'I lack experience,' Gabriel Angélico sighed in response to her descriptions.

Klara Jørgensen looked at him with gentle eyes.

'Experience just makes one restless, Professor. One can never get enough.'

She gave a slight toss of her head.

'Small dots on the great world atlas aren't dots any more after you've been there. They turn into feelings and atmospheres that you carry with you in your heart.'

'Is that painful?'

'No, you soon forget.'

'And the heart isn't that big either.'

'It isn't, is it?'

They sank back into silence, each with one arm on an armrest. However little or much was said during these evenings, each sentence lived on in its own echo, was rooted in the silence that followed and became immortal. Passers-by stopped in amazement at the sight of the tall black man and the foreign girl who conversed so familiarly but didn't look one another in the eye. It was an enigmatic sight, and in the belief that the two should not be disturbed, the people made long detours to leave them alone. Only in dark billiard halls, in the shade outside the liquor stores and at chemists' counters went the whisper that after years of enforced loneliness, life had finally been merciful to Gabriel Angélico.

During the day they carried on as before and never spoke together in the school courtyard. She fled past him on her way to the library, with her books under her arm and her hair brushed into a pony tail. He ceased entirely to look at her over the edge of his newspaper, because he knew perfectly well when she approached. The fear that she wouldn't notice him vanished too and was replaced by the anticipation of their evening meeting. He continued to teach her every day, but aimed as little comment in her direction as he'd previously done. Instead, he waltzed up and down in front of his desk as before, gesticulated enthusiastically with chalk and textbooks while his pupils guffawed obligingly. Even Klara Jørgensen smiled at him when, accidentally-on-purpose, he cracked his witticisms, but he never dared look in her direction and smile back. Only occasionally did he feel that he couldn't endure it all, that this mask concealing his melancholic nature was more and more constricting and that all he wanted to do was to rip it off, obliterate all these other bit-parts in the drama of his life, and take her by the arm in one theatrical exit. Of course it was unthinkable, their modes of expression couldn't encompass it, he couldn't do it to her. Not to her, she who never really looked him properly in the eyes, but always fixed her gaze on anything but him.

Then the evening would arrive and she would be under the olive tree once more. Gabriel Angélico was as uncertain as ever about how far he could enter into her private life. He had little idea how these moments by the river fitted into her twenty-three years of life before they'd come to know one another. Sometimes he wanted to ask her the simplest things, like who had given her the wrist-watch she sat fiddling with, what her bedroom had looked like when she was a child, how she dressed in the winter. She'd never mentioned her family, and he had no clue about why she'd chosen to leave them for this perverse equatorial clime. He didn't ask either, but let her say the things she wanted to. When Gabriel Angélico and Klara Jørgensen conversed at dusk, it was never the minutiae that came first, but the thoughts surrounding them, honed down into short sentences to soften their fall. Anything that might have given Gabriel Angélico an idea of Klara Jørgensen's former life was omitted, or camouflaged by something quite different.

On the other hand, Gabriel Angélico would sometimes tell Klara Jørgensen about his own family. They were, after all, so much nearer than hers, and sometimes she even caught a glimpse of them through the living-room window if she leant back a bit.

'My aunt dreams of going to Paris,' said the Professor with a faraway look. 'She dreams of drinking coffee out of small cups on the Left Bank of the Seine.'

'Yes, that's lovely,' said Klara Jørgensen.

'I don't understand,' said the Professor.

'What?'

'How coffee can taste different in one place than in another.'

'But it does, though.'

'Well, it's beyond me.'

Klara Jørgensen watched him with some sympathy.

'It's not really the coffee that's being drunk,' she said. 'Rather the atmosphere that goes with it.'

'You drink atmospheres?'

'Yes. It's the senses that go travelling.'

'But one forgets so easily.'

'Yes, that's true.'

She was silent for a moment.

'But that doesn't mean they vanish. Every impression is stored away somewhere in the memory and can be jogged by the smallest things.'

'What, for instance?'

She thought for a moment.

'Fried banana, perhaps. Down here people fry bananas all the time. I don't eat them. But I like the smell of them.'

Klara Jørgensen breathed in, as if she'd caught a whiff from Señora Yolanda's kitchen that had spread right down to the river.

Yolanda Archetti was born on Christmas Day 1955, as small boys sang carols outside her mother's window. She was an engaging child, and before she'd reached the age of fifteen, eight suitors had turned up on her doorstep. One after the other, bearing marbles and chocolate. The young Yolanda wasn't much interested in studying; instead her ambition was to leave Italy as soon as humanly possible. The only reason she remained in the small Italian town as long as she did was out of love for the three cats who followed her wherever she went. When Yolanda Archetti was twenty-one she was ambushed by a Father Christmas who turned out to be a sailor from North Africa in disguise. She lived with him for three years in Zimbabwe, after which she settled in the Greek islands with a Swedish botanist, in Eastbourne with a Scottish sociologist, and in Lisbon, where she shared a house with a former Russian spy who wrote crime novels based on conspiracy theories of the most convoluted kind.

As she approached her thirties she was working as a receptionist in a tourist hotel on the Spanish island of Tenerife. Here she met a portly Lebanese who earned his living selling tequila and a number of other cocktails he'd invented himself and named after his twelve siblings. The Lebanese was called Salman Yeti and had worked on the island for a dozen years. He was an oil worker by trade and had lived in Saudi Arabia for several years, but had grown tired of oil wells. He took a strong liking to the Italian woman, who'd filled out with the years and who now possessed a body of generous proportions. But Salman Yeti spoke very little Spanish and even less Italian, and he doubted that the delightful lady had any command of Lebanese. Eventually he talked the chamber maid into writing a note which said simply: *I like you. Would you consider going out with me one evening?* The message surprised Yolanda Archetti, who hadn't found the barman the least bit exciting. However, she accepted, for she too had physical needs that had to be met. And so it was that Salman Yeti and Yolanda Archetti had their first date one evening by the beach, speaking in sign language and through the offices of a most helpful waiter, who reddened more and more at the sentiments he was asked to convey.

No one could say for certain what made Yolanda Archetti marry a not very attractive Lebanese man at the age of thirty-two. It was almost certainly not her biological clock, which appeared to have stopped some time in the sixties. But still she took him as her husband, in a modest ceremony in southern Spain, before they both travelled to the Caribbean coast of South America, where Salman Yeti had landed a well-paid job as an inspector with the Venezuelan oil refineries. They settled in a small town in the Andes, in a beautiful villa where Yolanda Archetti passed her days running a small restaurant. Salman Yeti was rarely at home, but that didn't seem to worry the good-natured woman unduly. On the few occasions her husband returned, the neighbours were quick to manoeuvre into position on the other side of the garden fence, so that they could do their crochet and drink iced tea to the sound of the foreign couple's conversations. These were a mixture of Spanish and English, with the odd foreign exclamation thrown in, and spiced with the occasional peal of intense laughter. Nobody understood a word of this language the couple had evolved, but that only made it all the more entertaining. Not to mention the noises that emanated from the bedroom on the lower ground floor late in the evenings.

One morning Klara Jørgensen sat on the stairs to her room watching the cats steal up to their feeding bowls in the garden. She had learnt to recognise all thirty-three of them, as they all had completely different characteristics. One had been blue when it was found, another was completely blind. The big grey one always slept with her tongue sticking out. Now they were all waiting for Señora Yolanda, who was bending over their dishes, about to fill them. She looked up at the young girl on the stairs, as the cats wove like velvet threads about her feet.

'What are you thinking about, Miss Klara?' she asked.

Klara Jørgensen considered for a moment before rising to move closer.

'Señora Yolanda, have you had many suitors?'

Señora Yolanda wiped cat food from her hands and laughed. 'My goodness, yes. More than I care to remember.'

'And why did you choose Señor Yeti?'

Her landlady smiled and shook her head.

'I really have no answer to that.'

'Was he good-looking?'

'Good Lord no, from certain angles he looked like a hunch-back.'

'But was he amusing?'

'Perhaps, but in a language I couldn't understand.'

A deep furrow appeared on Klara Jørgensen's forehead.

'But what was it then?'

Señora Yolanda chuckled softly and seated herself on a rickety garden chair.

'He's good. He looks after me, and since he got rid of his moustache, he doesn't resemble a guerrilla leader quite so much.'

'And you're happy?'

'Yes, certainly. I've got this lovely house, my cats and a nice girl like you to keep me company. Why shouldn't I be happy?'

Klara Jørgensen went to fetch a jug of lemonade from the fridge and the two women sat in the garden with their eyes shut against the sun.

'There's something troubling you, isn't there, Miss Klara?'

Klara Jørgensen released a sigh the way young women often do.

'I feel so restless.'

Señora Yolanda chortled.

'That's hardly surprising. You travel the world like other people catch a bus.'

'I've been here a long time now.'

'Four months.'

'That's quite long.'

'Well, yes. I've been here for eleven whole years.'

'And you've never gone off anywhere?'

'No.'

'Don't you want to, either?'

'No. I'm fine where I am.'

Klara Jørgensen sighed once more.

'I wonder when that'll happen to me. When I'll stop having this craving to move on.'

'Maybe never.'

'But I want it to happen. Somewhere or other.'

Señora Yolanda opened her eyes.

'It's not the place that matters, my dear. You have to find someone you can live with. That's what matters.'

The landlady smiled and blinked in the sun.

'Remember, Miss Klara, that we don't build our homes in houses or flats, in landscapes or destinations. We take up residence within people and link our existence to theirs.'

Señora Yolanda gave the girl a calm look and then lay back.

'Just you wait,' she said.

And shortly afterwards she was asleep in her chair, while Klara Jørgensen sat quietly with a book in her hands reading the same page over and over again.

Both Gabriel Angélico and Klara Jørgensen knew that reality was about to catch up with them. Sometimes his mother would draw the living-room curtains back so that she could watch her son and the girl secretly. At other times she left the window open and tried to overhear the mumbling from outside. His sister would occasionally stick her head out of the front door and stand there looking at the back of their necks, imagining they didn't notice her. Passers-by gradually ventured closer before they veered off in another direction, curiosity driving them towards the house by the river, for by now the girl had been there so often that she'd begun to be harmless. People gossiped about her on the stone steps of the Iglesia de la Santisima Trinidad after morning mass, on the cracked marble benches in the park, in the queue at the baker's or over the domino board on Sunday mornings. The people of the little riverside quarter were as black as night, descendants of slaves that the Spaniards had brought with them, a little community of low brick houses and dirty little streets. No visitors or tourists or foreign students went there. No foreigners, except her. But by now they were becoming used to the sight of her and slowly but surely beginning to imagine that she belonged there.

Then the rain came. It came when Klara Jørgensen was crossing the bridge, on her customary route to the house by the river, when Gabriel Angélico had already seated himself in the shade of the olive tree to wait. The first raindrop fell on the tip of his shoe and the next hit his right cheek. His heart convulsed like an animal in its final death throes, because he knew what it meant. He'd never realised before that bad weather would spell the end of their liaison, that the rainy season would render it impossible for her to sit there, as the olive tree's branches were far from water-tight and there was no roof over the porch. But still he continued to wait until he heard her footfall on the damp gravel and sensed her sinking down beside him. The chair was already wet, but she didn't seem to worry about that. He turned to her and smiled, as the rain increased in strength.

'Your face is flushed,' he told her.

'I think I've got a temperature,' she said.

But she only smiled and let the droplets run off her hair and down her face.

'We can't sit here,' said Gabriel Angélico at last and made to get up.

At the same moment Klara Jørgensen caught hold of his hand. Her hot fingers rested on his brown knuckles without covering them completely. Gabriel Angélico thought he was going to melt away and die. He was lost for words, but he had no need of them, anyway. Because at that moment his grandmother appeared on the steps with an umbrella.

'In with the pair of you,' shooed Florentina Alba. 'You're tempting fate sitting out here.'

Klara Jørgensen rose slowly and looked at the old woman.

'Come in, my dear,' said his grandmother.

With a quick glance at the Professor, Klara Jørgensen held out her hand to Florentina Alba and let herself be led into the family home. Gabriel Angélico gulped twice and, with a stooping back, followed.

Ana Risueña insisted on packing Klara Jørgensen into a threadbare woollen blanket and serving her passion-fruit tea, which bewildered the visitor completely. They placed her on the sunken velvet sofa in the living-room, which must have been bought some time in the fifties. Young Alexandra dried her hair and asked if she could comb it, while Florentina Alba stuffed the girl's mouth with grapes, something that would guarantee the best of fortune. This evening all of Gabriel Angélico's family was to share in Klara Jørgensen's company. As if summoned to an audience with the bishop, they trooped along in the rain to exchange a few words with her. Victor Alba lit the fire, and the aunt who dreamt of Paris dug the candelabra out of the chest of drawers. A soup made from pigs' trotters was prepared, and Gabriel Angélico's fat uncle produced a bottle of home-made brandy. Mustafa brought along a red wine from Europe, but the heat had turned it to an unpalatable vinegar. So instead, he ran home and grabbed a bottle of Sambuca, tossed seven coffee beans into the bottom of the glass before lighting it and offering it to Miss Klara. She could only laugh at all the efforts to make her feel welcome. And she ate her pigs' trotters and drank glasses of moonshine and Sambuca, while Gabriel Angélico watched her stonily from his armchair.

They wanted to know all about her. It was an interrogation that lasted late into the evening, in which they went through everything, from what she ate for breakfast in her native land to what her bedroom looked like. Klara Jørgensen explained how one made brown bread with a dark crust, what books she had in her room, how long or short her winter coats were, what sort of footwear she used when it snowed, why frost mist looked just like any other kind of mist, where in the Norwegian metropolis the best hot chocolate was to be found, and what it felt like to look forward to spring. She described it all with enthusiasm in her voice and a hint of nostalgia. Gabriel Angélico noticed this too, and a shadow crept over his face. He noticed it most when she was describing her mother, who was fair of face and good and designed houses for people to live in.

And he tried to picture Klara Jørgensen's own existence, with charwomen and the like, soft bedclothes in every bedroom, a living-room full of thousands of books, and pictures on the walls that would obviously be expensive and beautiful. Wasn't it strange that now, just when she'd finally come into his home, she was on the point of slipping away from him again? She no longer belonged solely to him, but to a whole host of other beings. Even those closest to him asserted their right to her, as they sat asking her things.

'But tell me, Miss Klara, what on earth made you decide to come here to Venezuela?' Victor Alba asked all of a sudden.

Everyone in the room looked at Klara Jørgensen, who felt the hot tea scorching her tongue. She didn't answer at once, but wrapped her hands around her cup as she often did when she was cold.

'Chance,' she said simply and gave a friendly smile.

'Were there lots of other schools you could have chosen?' asked Ana Risueña.

'Yes, there were,' replied Klara Jørgensen. 'But I chose this one.'

'What made you choose it?' Mustafa wondered.

'A picture,' replied Klara Jørgensen. 'I thought the mountains looked beautiful.'

'Aren't there mountains where you live?' asked Alexandra.

'Yes,' said Klara Jørgensen. 'But they're low and easier to cross. That's where the difference lies.'

The people in the room smiled at her and she set her cup down on the table.

'It's about time I was going,' she said with a little nod. 'Thank you all for your kindness. I'm nice and warm now.'

Forentina Alba took her by the arm and accompanied her out into the hall. She handed her a broken umbrella and patted her on the cheek.

'The others can't see it, but I can,' said the old women in the light from the candles. 'You're in love with Gabriel.'

'Am I?' said Klara Jørgensen, her eyes glistening. 'I thought I was just feverish. Are you certain it's not the drinks?'

'Oh no. I recognise the symptoms,' said Florentina Alba. 'Look, my grandson's coming. Say goodbye now and come again soon.'

The old woman disappeared and Klara Jørgensen went out on to the front steps. Gabriel Angélico came gliding through the doorway and they stood beneath the umbrella in the lee of the olive tree.

'You've got a wonderful family,' she said to him with a tiny shiver.

'They're not normal,' said Gabriel Angélico.

'No, they're not, are they?'

She gave a quick smile and was about to leave him. But he reached out and took her hand warily, as a sign that she should stay.

'Miss Klara, tell me why you came here?'

Her face took on a dull expression, as if the rain clouds had settled in it.

'Is it that important?'

'Yes.'

'I don't know why I move about from one place to another. Restlessness, perhaps.'

'Miss Klara, I've fallen in love with you.'

Klara Jørgensen looked at him in horror and two short gasps

escaped from her chest, as if she was trying to quell some troublesome hiccups.

'You mustn't do that.'

She fixed him with her eyes, and for the first time he thought he glimpsed her whole being. Then she said quickly:

'I'm in love with someone else.'

The words fell on to the doorstep like the edge of fortune's guillotine. Gabriel Angélico grasped his breast to soften the black hoplessness of her words. He had lost, now he had said the accursed words and would always regret it. But did it really matter? He would lose anyway. That was his lot. There was no happy ending to the game life had arranged for him.

'Goodbye, Miss Klara,' was all he said.

'Goodbye, Professor,' she said sullenly.

Then she moved slowly backwards and for a second it looked as if she was crying. But it might just have been the rain on her face. Then she turned and disappered into the squalls with the umbrella like a collapsed tarpaulin over her head. Gabriel Angélico watched her go and felt his hands freeze into clenched fists. His mother appeared in the door and put a hand on his shoulder.

'I hope your girlfriend will come again soon,' she said.

'She won't come again. And she's no longer my girlfriend,' said Gabriel Angélico.

'What's that you're saying?' said his mother, astounded.

'She's no longer anyone I know,' he repeated. 'After Monday she'll be something quite different.'

'What?' asked Ana Risueña, totally confused.

With a bitter look on his face Gabriel Angélico replied:

'A student.'

Klara Jørgensen used up her few remaining pounds on a book she'd already read three times before. It was slim and consequently very cheap. She got ten pence change and dropped it into the collection box by the till, which went to some deserving charity or, perhaps, to the woman who sat there unsmilingly taking the money. People overtook Klara Jørgensen as she passed the Duty Free shop with its cartons of cigarettes in Christmas gift-wrapping. One or two of the passers-by collided with her, but she took no notice of them. She moved slowly, not the way people walk in airports even when they've got plenty of time, strolling along with a far-away look, listening to the voices over the loudspeaker. A hymn of destinations welled up beneath the roof – Paris, Milan, Helsinki, San Francisco, gate such-and-such. Klara Jørgensen smiled thinly, handed her bag to the man in the white shirt and placed her keys in a dark blue bowl. She slipped through the metal detector, gathered her possessions and, at the same leisurely pace, passed some children's drawings acclaiming Heathrow as the world's foremost centre for air traffic. Then she wandered down the wide expanse of floor that was flanked by yellow numbers; meek, *en route*, in a pageant of strangers.

She took her seat by the window a little aft of the wing. She folded her coat and placed it in the locker together with her bag of presents, before starting to read the book she had bought. Now and then she glanced at the stragglers who were still boarding, as if hoping they would all pass and allow her to read her book in peace. After a while someone came and sat down in the seat next to her. Klara Jørgensen didn't glance up at him, but she noticed that he opened a men's magazine with boats on the front cover and that he was wearing yachting shoes. It seemed a strange choice of footwear for the middle of winter; his feet must have been very cold. But she liked his hands and found herself staring at them for long periods. They were rugged with sturdy fingers, and looked out of place on the magazine's shiny cover.

'What was his name again? I've forgotten.'

The gravelly voice took her by surprise; he must have seen her glancing sidelong at his shoes.

'Whose?'

'The old man. I've forgotten what he was called.'

He nodded down at the novel she was holding in her hands, which she was now starting for the fourth time.

'Santiago,' she replied. 'Have you read it?'

'Yes,' he said. 'It's not very long.'

Only now did she raise her head a little and look up at him. His face was tanned by the sun and his shirt was a jovial blue. Klara Jørgensen thought his eyes were full of stories and wondered what such a rock of a man looked like when he cried.

'Have you been travelling long?' he asked.

'All my life,' she replied.

He smiled.

'I mean this time.'

'No. I've just been to London.'

'And what have you been doing in London a week before Christmas?'

She closed her paperback, using her index finger as an outsized bookmark between the pages.

'Visiting bookshops. Drinking tea. Strolling about.'

'No Christmas presents?'

'Yes, a few. Mainly books.'

There was a silence and for a moment she contemplated returning to her story.

'What about you?' she asked almost in spite of herself. 'Where have you come from?'

'The Caribbean,' he said.

'Where abouts?'

'Venezuela.'

'That's next to Colombia, isn't it?'

'That's right. East of Colombia, north of Brazil, south of the Caribbean.'

'And what does one do in Venezuela a week before Christmas?'

He smiled once more.

'Sail. All the year round.'

'You're a yachtsman, then?'

'Yes. Can you tell?'

'You've got the wind in your face.'

'Even now?'

'Yes. Where do you sail?'

'Off a small island on the coast.'

'Is it nice there?'

'Very nice.'

'And are the sunsets beautiful?'

'Extremely beautiful.'

She pursed her lips and looked out at the clouds whose edges were now tinged with pink. It struck her that he must be a good deal taller than her and perhaps a good deal older, too. He had the hands of an old man and she liked them.

'Is sailing difficult?' she asked slowly.

'It all depends on the conditions.'

'And how long will you stay on your island, Captain?'

'A while.'

He smiled at the title she'd bestowed on him and folded his magazine to put it in the seat pocket.

'Have you been to the Caribbean?'

'Yes, but only to those tourist spots.'

'And you've been travelling all your life?'

'Yes. And you?'

'Always.'

They let down their tables and were served a light evening meal and small bottles of wine.

'And what does a girl like you do in Norway when she's not travelling?' he asked.

'I study literature. At the university.'

'And what are these studies leading up to?'

'No idea. I enjoy reading, that's all.'

'Do you always travel alone?'

'Usually.'

'So you're plucky, in other words.'

The comment embarrassed her.

'As far as I'm concerned you need more pluck to find someone to travel with,' she replied.

'Yes, that's true.'

'Do you always travel alone as well?'

'Always,' he answered. 'It's not easy finding someone who wants to move in the same direction as you.'

'No, that's the trouble.'

She poked cautiously at the food with her fork, took a mouthful and chewed slowly.

'Are you going home for Christmas?' she asked at length.

'Yes. I'm staying until after New Year.'

'Do you enjoy Christmas?'

'Not especially. It's a lot of fuss, don't you think?'

'No, I love it.'

'Oh. Why?'

'The world is beautiful at Christmas. It's warm and bright, almost as if it wasn't real.'

'You should write stories, the way you talk,' he said. 'You put things so well.'

She laughed, rather more shrilly than usual.

'I'm not good with words,' he said.

'I see. Where do your talents lie?' she asked.

'In my hands. I can make things. And mend things that have fallen to bits.'

'I'd never be able to do that. My fingers are too little.'

She held one hand out in front of her and looked at it. As a natural reflex, he raised his own great hand and laid it over her slender fingers. He squeezed them and felt how cold she was against the warm skin of his palms.

He turned his head to smile at her, but seemed rather taken aback by her terrified expression. Then he released her hand and it fell back on to her thigh like a dead skin.

'You're right,' he said. 'They can't do much except hold a pen. But they're just right for that.'

Only then did Klara Jørgensen's horrified face melt into a smile.

Klara Jørgensen didn't make a habit of talking to strangers. Especially not on flights and certainly not with the person who happened to be sitting next to her. She had no need of new acquaintanceships which, by their very nature, were doomed to be of such short duration. And anyway, she preferred to read or watch the clouds, particularly if the weather was fine or the sunset was especially lovely. On this flight from London, a week before Christmas, the sunset was absolutely superb. But Klara Jørgensen didn't even notice it; her gaze was on the creases in this strange man's face, and all her attention was fixed on the words that fell from his lips. He sat there talking to her and touching her hand without asking permission. And Klara Jørgensen enjoyed it so much she almost didn't know herself.

They landed and he let her precede him out of the plane. At baggage reclaim they stood watching the suitcases float down the belt like dozing dromedaries in a dim light. A little way off Christmas carols were being played. Wreaths with red ribbons decked the walls. Klara Jørgensen tightly clutched the bag she had in her hand, while the strange Captain pulled her suitcase off the belt as she pointed it out. She put on the coat she'd had over her arm, and did up all the buttons except the very top one. Then he handed over her suitcase and they stood facing each other for a while, each knowing that at such moments one must do more than make mere conversation, or never speak again.

'What's your name?' he asked finally.

'Klara,' she replied. 'And yours?'

'William.'

They smiled at one another. The bag of Christmas presents nudged gently against the fabric of her coat.

'How old are you?' he asked.

'Twenty-one,' she said. 'And you?'

'Thirty-two.'

He looked a trifle mortified.

'Do you think that's old?' he asked.

'Yes,' she answered. 'But you're not.'

He smiled again, a little mournfully it seemed, as if it were already too late. They had reached the point where she had to go, and he had to continue to watch the suitcases that flowed past. In the stillness of the moment she looked down at his shoes.

'Your feet will be frozen,' she said.

'Yes,' he said. 'I'd forgotten how cold it is here.'

She nodded.

'It's easy to forget,' she said quietly.

Several seconds of silence followed.

'Well, it was nice meeting you,' she said and held out her hand.

'And you too,' he said.

And as she took his hand, a small electric shock coursed through Klara Jørgensen's body, like the sudden static from a woollen blanket. He, for his part, stood watching her go, and when he eventually grabbed his suitcase, it had already passed him four times. That night she dreamt of him and he of her; such are the workings of the subconscious. But neither of them thought about destiny or predetermination, just that they'd both felt something that they dearly wished would continue. And both the girl and the Captain were convinced that a continuation could not be helped by any kind of predestination, but had to be brought about by the utmost exertions on both their parts.

At this period Klara Jørgensen and her sister were living at home with their parents, and each day was filled with Christmas preparations. The house had once belonged to her grandparents and was large, with an alarming number of staircases which caused visitors some confusion at times. Neither of the girls was in much of a hurry to leave their childhood home, despite the fact that Klara Jørgensen's elder sister had been in a steady relationship for more than two years. As for Klara Jørgensen, she'd only been in love once but she couldn't remember if that had been a long time ago, or if it just felt that way. She had few friends, but those she did have were very close and they'd learnt to accept that she was a girl who thought much, but said little. Her parents' house was full of books and at an early age Klara Jørgensen had begun to help herself from the shelves. During her youth she'd systematically read all fifteen hundred books in the living-room, before attacking the bookcases in the basement where new volumes presented themselves in all their profusion. Her mother used to say that Klara Jørgensen spent half her life in a fictional world, and that the ability to evanesce into its minutiae was the quality she most envied in her daughter.

Five days before Christmas Klara Jørgensen emerged from the reading room in the Faculty of Arts, her right hand aching slightly. For four hours she had elucidated on literary theory in left-sloping calligraphy, pressing hard enough to copy through three layers of paper. The test was merely a small part-exam and Klara Jørgensen wasn't worried about the result. Feeling mildly tired, she clapped her books under one arm and munched a currant bun her mother had given her. At that moment she caught sight of a stranger at the bottom of the wide staircase. He was sitting on a black plastic chair to the right of the door, with his hands behind his head. He smiled, and just then she knew who it was.

'Here's the student of literature,' the Captain said playfully.

'Is it you?'

'It certainly is.'

She halted in front of him and felt her cheeks beginning to burn.

'Well, what an amazing coincidence,' she said.

'Far from it. I've been sitting here for three hours.'

'Oh.'

'I phoned the faculty. They told me the literature students had their exam today.'

'And so you came to sit on that chair and wait for me?'

'Yes.'

'I see you've got some better footwear.'

'I bought them today. D'you like them?'

He swung out his feet with their brown boots.

'Yes.'

'What have you been writing about today?'

'All the great authors of the world.'

'Tell me, why don't you write yourself?'

'I haven't a lot to write about.'

'No?'

'No, nothing much has happened to me.'

He smiled and got up. On the way out he opened the door and let her go first, with a light touch on the small of her back that she scarcely felt through the lining of her jacket.

'You haven't lived all that long, after all,' he said.

'If I lived to be a hundred, I'd still be unable to write a book about it,' she said.

'Well, I wouldn't know. I don't read books.'

'Don't you read?'

He shook his head and kicked at the loose snow as they walked down towards the car park.

'I don't read novels.'

'What about *The Old Man and the Sea*?'

'Yes, that's about the only one I've read. Because it's about the sea. And because it's so short.'

He chuckled.

'I was lucky there,' he added.

Klara Jørgensen scrutinised him the way people examine a museum exhibit.

'So what do you read?' she asked.

'Travelogues,' he answered.

'Real ones?'

'Yes. That's just it. They're real.'

'But reality is so boring,' she sighed.

'Not always. It depends which part of it you move about in.'

She shook her head lightly and her black woolly hat almost fell off.

'I can see you haven't much to contribute on the subject of books,' she said.

'No,' he said, giving her a sideways glance. 'But maybe I can do something else.'

'Oh?' said Klara Jørgensen.

'Yes,' said the Captain. 'Maybe I can give you something to write about.'

For three days in succession William Penn invited Klara Jørgensen out to dinner, each time at a different restaurant. She waited for him in her parents' living-room with feigned indifference, suspecting him of seeking her company simply because it was outside the sailing season and he was bored. Her parents asked all sorts of questions about this man who came driving up in his father's black car, but she never gave a proper answer and simply disappeared down the steps with a vaguely sceptical expression on her face as soon as the bell rang. So, Knut and Ingeborg Jørgensen had to be content to watch their daughter cross the yard in front of the garage with a tall and well-dressed man who always opened the door for her. Klara Jørgensen used to look at his hands as they drove, those great working hands sanded by rigging and etched by the sea. Sometimes she wanted to feel them again, to feel if warmth would permeate the thick layer of skin on his palms, as it had that time on the plane when he'd touched her.

She liked to listen to him telling stories. They were mainly about boats. William Penn had been at sea all his life. As a small boy, his father had taken him out in a dinghy he'd built himself, and when the lad was fifteen he'd been given a small boat of his own. William Penn never got on well at school and instead, at sixteen, he joined the crew of a tanker and sailed round the world not once, but twice. When he was eighteen he got the chance to lose his virginity at a brothel in Shanghai, but the hang-ups of youth had caused him to decline. Later he'd returned home with the ideal woman in his head, but he'd never found her. Instead he'd moved in with the woodwork teacher's daughter and shared a house with her for two years. This was one of three more lengthy relationships, the last of which had gone on for five years and ended with him getting the lunatic idea of going to the Caribbean and settling on an island no one had even heard of.

On the fourth evening William Penn invited Klara Jørgensen to the opera. The Captain had no feeling for theatre, but he loved to hear operatic divas singing the Italian classics. Klara Jørgensen tried to understand what these histrionic females were singing about, but soon had to give up. She sent the Captain a sideways glance and discovered that his weather-beaten cheeks sported two lonely tears.

'Captain,' she whispered. 'You're crying.'

'I know,' he answered. 'It's her voice. It's so lovely.'

Klara Jørgensen's brow became deeply furrowed as she gazed down at the soprano who was singing out her sorrow.

'More lovely than average?' she whispered.

'Yes. She's exceptional.'

Klara Jørgensen's forehead contracted even further. She acknowledged privately that she was envious of the woman before them, who could get a man to weep and call her exceptional, just like that. Klara Jørgensen couldn't recall anyone shedding tears for her in a similar fashion.

'I can't understand what she's singing,' she whispered.

'No,' said the Captain and smiled. 'It doesn't matter, anyway.'

Klara Jørgensen giggled softly and felt strangely relieved when the lady with ringlets sank down dead on her highest note. The Captain brushed his hand rapidly across his face and gave a soft laugh.

After the performance they walked out together into the arcade outside the opera, where a Russian quartet was playing Christmas carols on oversized brass instruments. William Penn calmly placed his scarf around Klara Jørgensen's neck, because he could see she was cold. After that he lit a cigarette with his great hands, inhaled and looked at her with a smile that spread over his entire face.

'Did you enjoy that?' he asked.

'It was beautiful, but incomprehensible,' answered Klara Jørgensen.

'Exactly. That's exactly it. I've no idea what was going on, but look how red my eyes are.'

She had to smile at him, the corners of her mouth reluctant as usual.

'What makes you cry, Klara Jørgensen?' he asked.

'Words,' she replied.

'Then I must learn to be more eloquent,' he said.

'And I'll have to learn to sing,' she said.

He laughed contentedly and bent carefully towards her. And as the cigarette slipped from his fingers and lay glowing unnoticed on the ground, William Penn leant forward and kissed Klara Jørgensen's cold lips.

As the old year turned into the new, Klara Jørgensen stood

leaning against the railings of a balcony that faced the old town houses in Bjerregaardsgate. A spray of rockets lit up the sky overhead. People next to her raised their glasses in a toast, the cascades from the rockets crackled, someone shouted their resolutions into the frosty night. One or two others passed by and pecked her on the cheek, as she cringed under their touch. Klara Jørgensen held the old railings tightly as she tipped her head back and her eyes formed a matt background to the brilliant display that flickered within them.

'You're so quiet, Klara,' said a tall youth who came up with champagne in both hands. He was a childhood friend, one of the people she knew from way back.

'I'm always quiet,' she replied.

'Yes, but more so tonight.'

'I'm missing someone.'

'I wouldn't have believed that of you.'

'No, it's funny, isn't it?'

'Well, who is he?'

'He sails,' she said.

'As we speak?'

'No.'

'Where is he tonight?'

She sighed and smiled wanly.

'Not here.'

Then she took one of the glasses of champagne, lit a long, black lady's cigar and drank a toast with her friend. For a moment she considered confiding her yearning to him, but decided he'd almost certainly say the Captain was too old for her, and that wasn't the advice she wanted. They stood in silence on the balcony, while Klara Jørgensen thought about

William Penn who hadn't phoned her that day, although he'd phoned her every other day over Christmas. Without a call from him this day felt completely empty and devoid of meaning. In that moment, Klara Jørgensen realised she had become fond of William Penn. And she sighed in the certainty that if he didn't ring tomorrow either, she would regard that day as wasted too, and begin to wait for the next.

William Penn arrived on Klara Jørgensen's doorstep on New Year's Day with a bouquet of white roses in one hand. She did her utmost to stifle the enthusiastic smile that lit up her face when she saw him.

'Not very original, perhaps,' he said, handing her the roses.

'Unless one's never been given flowers before,' she answered, allowing the smile to break out a fraction.

'Shall we go for a walk?' he asked.

'OK. Let me get my coat.'

She showed him into the hall, and he stood looking at a family photograph above the row of hooks on the wall.

'What were you like as a child?' he asked her.

'Quiet,' replied Klara Jørgensen.

She buttoned up her coat, wound a scarf around her neck and pulled on her boots. They went out into the sharp light that made them screw up their eyes, each wearing gloves and smooth soles.

'I haven't known you very long,' said William Penn, taking her hand.

'Fifteen days,' she replied.

He laughed.

'I didn't know you were a quiet child, for example.'

'Well, you know now.'

'I do, don't I?'

They halted at the same moment, without warning.

'You're leaving soon, aren't you?' she said, looking at him with her mouth half covered by the thick scarf.

'Yes,' he said. 'Will you miss me, Klara?'

She looked down at her boots.

'Yes,' she mumbled, as if she didn't really want him to hear her answer.

'Klara,' he said, laying his hands gently on her shoulders.

'Yes.'

'Could you contemplate living on an island you've never heard of with a man you hardly know?'

Klara Jørgensen's mouth turned up in a smile and she gave a little laugh.

'Yes. I could.'

William Penn let out a small sigh, as if he'd practised holding his breath for longer.

'You're a strange creature,' he said as he hugged her close.

'Aren't I exceptional?' she enquired.

'Yes,' he said, laughing. 'You are exceptional.'

'Good.'

She would really have liked to see him cry too, but that would have to wait for another time.

'When do we have to leave?' she asked.

'Soon,' he said.

'I'll have to wait a bit,' she said. 'I've got another exam.'

'When?'

'Soon.'

'Then you can follow later,' he said, grinning.

Klara Jørgensen smiled once more. She had smiled far more this Christmas than normal. William Penn scrutinised her and thought her eyes were shining in child-like anticipation.

'Are there pelicans there?' she asked eagerly.

'Hundreds of pelicans,' he replied.

'And palm trees?'

'Everywhere you look.'

'And trees with oranges on?'

'Yes, and lemons and mangoes, too.'

'And are the beaches white?'

'Yes, clean and white and soft.'

'And the sunsets?'

'The loveliest in the world. At least according to the tourist brochure.'

She laughed in a way that wasn't in the least typical of her and a ray of light sprang from her dark pupils. In that instant William Penn realised that Klara Jørgensen obviously hadn't understood what she'd promised him that winter's day. He saw that this journey seemed no different to her than the daily one she made into a fictive world, that she had no inkling of how much learning to live in a place might alter her entire being. And yet he wanted to take her with him, he wanted to look after her and give her the fairytale world she expected. Anything, that she might be able to keep the clear gaze she'd turned on him, that no one might sully it and beat the truth into her breast. That life might not harden her, as it had hardened him, so imperceptibly that he could no longer remember when or how it had happened.

Colonel Edgar Penn had lost a leg in Italy during the Second

World War. During a bombing raid on one of the smaller villages he had rescued a young woman from a well. Afterwards he stayed with her family in the hope that his leg would heal of its own accord. He was bewitched by the girl's beauty, as well as her culinary skills, which proved to be miraculous at a time when few ingredients were available. Later, when his leg had to be amputated, he chose to remain several more months in the house where the girl could nurse him. Soon he fell in love with her, and she with him. As soon as peace descended on the continent of Europe, he hurried back to the village to woo her. They were married shortly afterwards, and had since been together for more than forty years. The colonel still found his wife beautiful, with her white hair gathered into a long plait on her back, and he still found her faltering English charming. And after he got a job at the British embassy in Norway, they both found themselves fumbling their way into a foreign language.

No sooner had Leonora Bigotti di Penn heard that her son was going to populate his island with a girl, than she invited the entire Jørgensen family to Bomannsvik. It was early January, and the boughs of the apple trees hung sullen and close to the ground, weighed down with wet snow. They ate in the summer-house, in which the colonel had installed a small fireplace, so it was like sitting out in nature's winter landscape. Leonora Bigotti served the loveliest pasta and veal with parmesan, together with goodly quantities of well-aged wine she had taken from her cellar. The colonel moved about, still healthy and masterful, despite being short of a leg again since becoming allergic to his own prosthesis fifteen years earlier. The atmosphere at table was very informal, the food went round in a never-ending carousel of eating, talking, laughter and dish-swapping. They were like neighbours who for a long time had lived at opposite ends of a long street, but who only now had taken the plunge and become acquainted.

Klara Jørgensen leant towards her sister at the corner of the table and whispered in her ear:

'Anyone would think we were engaged.'

Both sisters looked at the two sets of parents. Klara Jørgensen couldn't quite decide if she thought William Penn belonged more to their generation or her own, but decided that he didn't seem nearly so adult when they were alone together. It was only now, as he sat at a well-laid table doing all the correct things, that he appeared so much older than herself. Though from time to time he would look at her with a concealed smile, as if what he wanted to do more than anything was lift her out of her chair and carry her off to some lonely corner of the world.

The Captain took his coat and got up to have a cigarette out in the garden. He stood beneath the snow-sprinkling apple trees blowing smoke into the air, while she sat between her parents and watched him, coffee cup in hand. Everything she saw pleased her, the broad hands with the cigarette between two fingers, the calm look. And she thought that she really didn't know this man, that it would be years before she knew him the way she wanted to, but that it was a task she might as well begin right away. As she sat resting her eyes on him, she felt tranquil, as if the tense fear she occasionally experienced in his presence was in the process of receding. Just then her mother leant towards her and nodded at the other side of the table to where her sister and his elderly parents sat roaring with

119

laughter across generations, nationalities and the thumb-print of history.

'Isn't it extraordinary,' said Ingeborg Jørgensen. 'The small coincidences that bind us human beings together.'

Gabriel Angélico was absent for days without anybody noticing. The rain that had arrived with the thunderstorm continued to inundate the streets and houses between the mountains until people had to close their shutters and lock themselves in. The school was shut temporarily because the courtyard with its parrot cages resembled a dock in which almond blossom, used pencil stubs and the holy Virgen de Fatima floated round in everlasting eddies. In the avenue outside, buses fought their way on against both current and geography, while rubbish and lost property sailed past on its way downstream, until someone chanced to pick it up. The market stalls were covered in gloomy tarpaulins, and the sky loured in all its gravity. People dragged their savings and empty shopping bags to the supermarket to hoard whatever they could. The air turned heavy, thickening like a simmering sauce, until it was unbearable to breathe. Cockroaches and small frogs came creeping in through gaps beneath doors and cracks in walls and settled in kitchen cupboards and wash-basins. The trees in the parks bent their heads as the worst of the squalls whipped down, and suburban flower-beds were washed out into the streets to blacken the tarmac. The rain eased and increased, but never stopped, and the only people who ventured from door to door were the umbrella salesmen, who were doing good business at last.

Even Ana Risueña didn't notice her son's absence. She had more than enough to do keeping the water away from her own doorstep. Although the river had long since broken its banks and was oozing and trickling in through cracks and crevices in the old brick building, she had succeeded in preventing any serious flooding. The olive tree now stood with its roots in water, while its boughs seemed to be weighed down with self-pity. Occasionally, some object would come drifting past the high doorsteps, an old post-box come adrift, billiard balls that had been shot out into the streaming streets, a lonely crucifix with the Saviour floating on his back. Ana Risueña stood with folded arms at the kitchen window watching this judgement from God which had descended on them without warning. Alexandra was in bed, because rain had a tendency to make her ill, and she slumbered, mildly delirious, through it all. Had these necessities not demanded Ana Risueña's full and undivided attention, she might have noticed that both her son and the two chairs from the front of the house were missing. No trace of them remained, the waters had washed away the Professor's footprints and the marks left by the chairs he'd taken with him. Perhaps Ana Risueña thought that these had been swept away in the storm as well, the way everything else seemed to vanish with the torrents of nature. And if anyone had asked her where her son was, she would presumably have replied that he, too, had floated away with the rain-water.

Klara Jørgensen rose from her bed feeling that she'd forgotten something important. The storm had raged for several days and the rain hadn't even ceased during the night. Nature's murkiness made the room almost dark, as if the sorrows of the entire world hung over it. She got up and walked barefoot to the steps that were smooth with rain-water. The droplets moistened her forehead and lips, they ran slowly down her solemn cheeks and disappeared inside the collar of her nightdress. Even her chest gurgled, like some soporific swamp where everything bubbles, but is never really released. The feeling of wakefulness was strange, as if she'd accustomed herself to wandering about like a sleep-walker. She lifted her hand and wiped sodden flower pollen from her brow before going back in, shutting the door and throwing off her nightdress. Naked, she crossed to the bed and picked up a crumpled postcard that had fallen down and ended up beneath it. It was in the clumsy scrawl of the man who sailed on the coast and who was still waiting for her. She shook the dust from it and put it to her face so she could smell the long-forgotten tang of the sea. Then Klara Jørgensen dressed and went out in the rain with an umbrella and sandals.

In the street she passed unkempt stray dogs that looked like rumpled rugs someone had forgotten to bring in. On the verandas, safely in the dry, people sat in rocking chairs and hammocks as they stared at the rain that continued to keep them off the streets. In the avenue, the baker stood behind his counter as the smell of newly baked corn-cakes turned into a strange, humid stink as it escaped from his shop. The water gouged tunnels in the flower beds between the benches in the square and no one had remembered to switch off the fountain that now resembled a running bath in the middle of the townscape. People no longer looked one another in the eye in these drab surroundings. If they ventured out of doors, they passed each other sighing beneath pristine umbrellas and noticed nothing more than new puddles and dripping palm boughs. Only the very few who owned gumboots went to mass, because the square in front of the cathedral resembled a small lake, and no one thought God had intended them to receive his blessing without dry feet.

Klara Jørgensen waded up the hill to the airport. At the entrance to the main hall, where the taxis usually waited, she folded her umbrella and glanced at the empty desks. The place was completely deserted, not a single plane had landed or taken off during the past few days. Even so, she walked past the rows of shiny chairs which dumbly displayed their emptiness, while her sodden sandals slapped at the floor, as if she was moving about in a marsh. At the far end of the hall one lonely, blue-uniformed individual sat behind a counter. The woman was alone at work today. The airline which employed her was the country's largest and had learnt a thing or two from the Americans; they went to work regardless of the weather. She gave Klara Jørgensen a relieved smile, as if for one moment she'd thought she was the only person left on earth. Klara Jørgensen replied with a tiny smile in return.

'Are there any departures to Vidabella?' she asked.

'It's very unlikely,' answered the woman. 'You'd do best to fly to the coast and then take the ferry.'

Klara Jørgensen nodded and pulled out a wallet from her wet bag.

'A ticket to Puerto la Cruz, please,' she said.

'When would you like to travel?'

'As soon as possible.'

'Do you want a return ticket?'

'No thanks.'

The woman glanced up for a moment or two, as if questioning whether the girl really had no intention of coming back.

'Obviously I can't guarantee a departure to that destination, either,' said the woman. 'Not if this weather continues.'

Klara Jørgensen nodded and placed the ticket in her bag together with her change. Water was dripping from her fringe and on to her shoes.

'It so seldom rains here,' the woman said apologetically.

'True,' replied Klara Jørgensen. 'But when it gets going, it's unendurable.'

She gave a little nod and began to make for the exit again. The woman watched the foreign girl with a certain curiosity and sympathy. A tourist, doubtless, and the despair in her eyes had to be measured against the misfortune of ending up here just as the town had become a landscape of water and cloud. It was understandable enough that she had no desire to return in sunnier weather.

The world stood still for a moment, as if the universe had paused to draw breath. The buses cancelled their departures and businesses closed, the baker turned off his oven and threw the left-overs to the ducks which came swimming from all directions of their new El Dorado. Taxi drivers parked their taxis in garages and wound up the windows. Petrol stations put plastic covers over their pumps and pulled down the metal shutters of their shop windows. The cafés froze their cakes and emptied their coffee-machines, while upturned chairs pointed their legs akimbo from the edges of tables. The painters vanished from Calle de los Pintores, and the sound of the *empanadas* women and newspaper vendors gradually died away as they crept back to their homes. Church doors slammed with a heavy thud, and the banks turned off their calculators and locked away their money. No dog barked in the streets any more, no cat smuggled itself softly through the blackness of night. It was as if the whole town lay in torpor, as if the mountains were comatose and the people hypnotised. They sat in their living-rooms drinking rum and watching soaps on television all day long, until the link with the antenna in the mountains was cut and they ended up just drinking rum and telling the same old stories over and over again.

In her room, Klara Jørgensen began to pack away her life. She wanted to leave in a week's time, weather permitting. It was sooner than she'd planned, but the end-of-term ceremony at the school would be a protracted affair anyway. Her final assignment lay completed on the desk by the window. A study of Cervantes' *Don Quixote* with emphasis on the characters' inner development. It had been written out of duty and in boredom, to the sound of rain sweeping the roof tiles, and not with her usual eagerness and enthusiasm. No story seemed to absorb her any more, they all seemed devoid of content, flat and full of banalities. Working her way into the romantic tragedies, the unspoken melancholy or doleful destinies of others no longer held any attraction for her. All she heard when she opened a book and let her gaze run down its pages, pages completely choked with letters, was the irritating sound of her own heart. The hammering at her temples, the thudding in her chest, her wrists vibrating and disturbing her, all made concentration impossible, and only with the greatest effort was she able to complete her work.

In the evenings she would sometimes sit and contemplate her own reflection in the mirror. Her face seemed unfamiliar, as if in reality she hadn't known what it looked like. It was only now she noticed it was thin and almost lifeless, not cool and unsullied as she'd imagined. Her smooth skin seemed to have coarsened under the sun, she had lines round her eyes she'd never seen before. The past year seemed to have worked on her skin the way time ravages a mountainside. She was no longer as young as she'd thought. Instead, she'd developed small pimples on her cheeks, her eyes had sunk and crevices had formed beneath them, her brow was shiny and her jaw line heavier. Her pupils had darkened, as if blackened with sorrow. Not the unfounded mournfulness of her youth, but a sadness only adults can harbour, that comes with the years, takes hold and grows into the body. The face in the mirror was no longer part of the image she'd had of herself, the carefree girl with her wary smile and restless being. Something had changed. Her smile was different, it had acquired the slight echo of melancholy and experience, a breath of bleak despair.

And then, as if with a breath, it lifted. The clouds rolled away, and the transparent sky came into view. Doors were thrown open, water evaporated from the streets, and the sand dried beneath people's feet. The vegetable sellers came running to the market with their wares, which the rain had made more plentiful than ever. The town revived, the trees reached out their branches as a sleeper stretches his waking arms. Everywhere things began to blossom, people smiled, they emerged from their bolt-holes and greeted each other happily in the streets. Corners sported the same regulars, and again there arose from the bakeries the smell of roasted coffee beans and melted cheese. The shops opened their doors wide and celebrated with tempting offers, while cakes flouted themselves like newly-baked flirts on the café shelves. Once more schoolchildren came running with freshly laundered socks and rattling school bags, again the sound of aircraft propellers could be heard in the morning, and there was a sigh of relief now that the outside world had found its way in through the gateway of cloud.

The institute opened its doors and called its students back to their classrooms. Klara Jørgensen tramped up in worn jeans clutching her final assignment tightly in her hand. The door to the reception room swung back and forth across the doorstep and she halted a moment out of old habit and glanced at the time-cards. She didn't dare dwell too long on them, but walked on, past the cleaning woman and a flood-damaged virgin, as the parrots' squawking and the newly re-kindled laughter of students reached her from the courtyard. Instead of going closer she turned to the right and went up the stairs to the classrooms. There, she stood in the doorway staring at her own desk in the back row by the window. Silently she went over and seated herself, propped her chin on her hand and looked out. She sat thus for a long while, as the rows of desks filled with the same old faces exchanging the usual words with each other. She sat still, and then she heard footsteps approaching from out in the corridor. She felt her heart was about to fill the entire room from floor to ceiling, like some swollen, over-ripe tomato that the heat had ravaged.

A short, green-eyed man came in and took up position in front of the blackboard. He gave a fleeting smile and his name, before explaining why he'd come. Unfortunately, Professor Angélico was not able to be there that day, and the man with green eyes had offered to fill his place. He then asked the students to get out their assignments so that he could gather them in and take them home for marking. The lesson was concluded soon afterwards, which delighted the students, and once again they headed out for the sun. Only Klara Jørgensen remained. She sat quietly in her chair long after the teacher and the last student had left the room, and only small, cryptic letters remained on the blackboard in the shade of the world atlas hanging in front of it. Her head no longer rested on her hand but supported itself, and her lower lip quivered slightly. She felt chilled, as her shoulders contracted in short, slight shudders. All she could do was go on looking out of the window; that was the simplest thing, to turn her head away. Because if anyone came in now she would have to shut her eyes for an instant, blink just for a moment. Klara Jørgensen sat and cried, and for the first time she knew exactly where these tears came from.

Gabriel Angélico didn't show up the next day or the day after that. At school they said he was sick, but no one really knew what was the matter with him or where he was. Nor did it seem that many people cared much. In spite of his popularity with the students, very few could be bothered to ask after him. Instead, they noted his absence with indifference between yawns of boredom and resigned themselves to the idea of putting up with some casual replacement. Gabriel Angélico was like a comic who has suddenly been axed from the revue. He was forgotten as a theatrical success; his was a voice that had elicited laughter, certainly, but one which had possibly forgotten that laughter is of such ephemeral and merciless brevity: it doesn't sit in the breast like tears. The world sighed only half-heartedly over Gabriel Angélico's disappearance. His time-card remained mutely on the wrong side of the clock with more and more vacant days on it.

Still no one had asked about him after Gabriel Angélico had been absent for a week. He rarely visited the shops, didn't drink, was never ill and never went to church. The Professor had always spent his evenings down by the river, usually in the shadow of his own room, but more recently on the chair next to her. Everyone noticed that Klara Jørgensen came no more, and speculation about her sudden departure was rife under every electric fan in the valley. But no one wondered about Gabriel Angélico. They assumed he had just gone into his house and remained there, writing away at his novels, those manuscripts no one would ever read, but which occupied all his time when he wasn't teaching. The Professor was only essential to a small handful of people and they had seen him vanish before, in search of a view of the sea or any view other than the usual one.

'I only hope he isn't ill,' Ana Risueña said to her old mother.

'Of course he isn't ill,' replied Florentina Alba. 'Unless life itself is an illness.'

Only one person seemed to feel the loss of Gabriel Angélico. This person stood in front of the clock in the mornings, with arms limp, staring at his card. She kept hoping she'd find it on the other side, and her face fell when it was still untouched and covered with dust. Nobody noticed her brittle glances, for no one at the school knew that she and the Professor had ever exchanged more than a casual word. Nor did they notice her furtive glances at the chair beneath the parrot cage where he used to read the newspaper, or at the blackboard where someone else now scribbled out his wisdom in quite a different way. In all these things there was nothing left for Klara Jørgensen. Nothing in the trees' shade, nothing in the long corridors or amongst the sighing rows of desks, nothing in the room above the tiled roofs of the bourgeoisie. But no one noticed this, because her loss went as unheeded as when dumbness descends on a silent person.

Klara Jørgensen began to dream about Gabriel Angélico at night. In her sleep she would take him to the sea. There they would sit on the seafront of Puerto la Cruz, on a small veranda with well-nurtured pot-plants and rattan chairs, by a small table with a linen tablecloth. They would sit there drinking anisette and facing the sunset while during the day a boat would take them out to islands where they would lie on the sand. Here, Gabriel Angélico was at last able to dip his feet into the water. She wanted to teach him to swim and float on his back, teach him to watch out for currents and waves, not to hurt his feet on the stones or swim too far out. She wanted to take him to one of the Italian restaurants where the chef played the violin and the waiters sang, and let him gorge himself on languid steaks, tepid wine and olives, and watch his eyes grow as he looked at her. And they would forget all other realities than these, lick ice-creams at lop-sided tables on the promenade and stroll in the light of the lamps on the bandstand, watch the lobster that lumbered up and down in the tank by the pavement restaurant and sniff the aroma of incense spreading out across the horizon. And at night she would sit up and watch over him sleeping, beneath a sheet that smelt of starch and hot irons, while the moment hung fast in the mechanism of time and halted all forward motion.

Each morning she awoke to disappointment. It was with a certain surprise that Klara Jørgensen acknowledged her unhappiness. The feeling was foreign to her. She bore her sadness like a tunic; it hung chill against her body and made her cold. All her senses complained in quiet unison over Gabriel Angélico. He was the only thing that occupied her thoughts, and anyone who drew her attention away from him made her irritable. Señora Yolanda was taken aback by the girl's shortness and abruptness, at the way she withdrew even more into herself, as if she had lost all contact with her earthly surroundings. Klara Jørgensen stopped making her bed, stopped reading her books, stopped talking to anybody at all. But every evening she sat at the top of the stairs outside her room and smoked, not one cigarette, but ten maybe, until she felt sufficiently sick and nauseous to sleep. In the mornings she went up to the institute to see if Gabriel Angélico had come, but soon returned home again despondent and ate just half a corn-cake for lunch, which she stared at in disgust. Then she wandered round the garden with the cats at her feet, not speaking to anyone and with a look that seemed as if it was retreating further and further into her own body.

By the time Gabriel Angélico had been missing for a fortnight, Ana Risueña began to be alarmed. Her son had no money and she was worried he wasn't eating. If she'd had any notion of where he might be, how far he'd dragged the two chairs, she would have gone to him now and asked him to come home. But she didn't know where to look, she wasn't fit after all the hours spent on steps or in the velvet suite in the living-room, and wasn't capable of setting out to rescue anyone. When she enquired about Gabriel Angélico in the streets, everyone gave the same answer, that the last time they had seen him he had been sitting in front of the house by the river with the foreign girl, although they'd not set eyes on her since the rains began. And then they'd mumble something about how they ought to go down to the house again soon and say hello, before they shuffled off in their slippers and patterned wraps and hair-clips like small antennae sticking out of their heads.

The weary woman sought refuge in Mustafa's bar. Ana Risueña perched on a high wooden stool and leant her elbows on the counter amongst lollies, vanilla-flavoured biscuits and American chewing-gum. Mustafa went to the cooler and got a bottle of soda which he placed before her with a straw in it. On the wall leading to the cooler were clippings from Pakistani newspapers and pictures of mosques of the world, together with a strip of Marilyn Monroe in a variety of swimming costumes. The counter was long and narrow and covered with the nicks and scratches of restlessness, the earth floor was full of small hollows, and the awning above the open door at the end let only a thin wedge of light into the premises. The walls were covered with home-made shelves on which anisette and rum were stacked in brown and plain glass bottles, together with a few rows of cheap whisky and Sambuca. Like the good Muslim he was, Mustafa never drank, and although profits from the addictive stuff weren't strictly in accordance with the Holy Book, he comforted himself with the thought that at least he gave infidels something to drown their sorrows in. He had his regulars who hung about on the corner all the time, until some novice of a police constable chased them away. But Ana Risueña was rarely there. He thought it best to offer her something that would first and foremost quench the thirst, but not necessarily anaesthetise the pain in her drawn face.

'You look like you've got the weight of the world on your shoulders,' he said to her as he swung the handle of his till.

'My son has vanished,' said Ana Risueña.

'Most definitely not. God knows where he is.'

'True,' sighed the woman. 'The Lord sees everything and knows everything, but he doesn't do much about it.'

'Well, at least he'll be looking after the Professor.'

Ana Risueña shrugged her shoulders.

'Gabriel will be all right. He's in love. That sort of thing doesn't make you ill.'

Mustafa nodded calmly as he tipped a splash of rum into the narrow neck of the bottle in front of the Professor's mother. Then he got down on to a crumbling mat, facing Mecca, to pray.

A shadow came gliding down the river valley that same afternoon. It was a shadow from the sun and not the coming darkness, a fair head that made the occasional observer nod in recognition from behind a ragged curtain. At the entrance to his bar, Mustafa knew immediately the blue dress and the slender face reddened by the sun. He watched her pass in a formation of road dust and sighed at the thought that she no longer had anyone to visit. Not wishing to lose sight of her, he put one foot outside the door and followed her attentively with his eyes.

'She's come,' he mumbled to Ana Risueña, who was still hunched on the bar stool.

'At last,' said the mother.

Together they went out and followed the girl. By the time they reached the house by the river they had almost caught up with her, believing that there she would stop. But Klara Jørgensen halted only a moment in front of the empty steps, now bereft of their two chairs. Instead of waiting there she walked on, her eyes lifted to the wooded hillsides in front of the house. They saw her disappear into the scrub by the river's edge, take off her trainers at the stepping stones and wade through the gurgling waters to the far bank. With arms folded, Mustafa raised his head to watch her as she slowly climbed the hillside, without shoes on her feet or any other kind of protection.

For two weeks Gabriel Angélico had been talking to the angels. He had been cross-examining them endlessly about why such a warm enchantment should be superseded by this most diabolical desperation. Life had caressed his brow, only to slap him in the face the moment after. Now he'd been left with a wounded soul; no, it had been irreparably damaged and could never be the same again. In small, short snatches of time he'd had everything he wanted. Suddenly life took it all back. Gabriel Angélico had never felt himself poorer, more miserable. But could it really be that one spark of happiness was to last an entire lifetime? No, he couldn't believe it. He couldn't have waited so long for something that was so fleeting. Oh, yes he could, said reality, giving him another sock in the face with its best gloves on. Gabriel Angélico had had what was due to him and now that he'd glimpsed it, he couldn't bear the thought of mourning it for the rest of his life.

He was hungry and exhausted, but he was insensible to it. He was scorched by lightning and stiff with rain, but his body didn't feel it. Every sensation he had was suffused with loss, was etched into the empty chair he'd placed by his side and which was her space. He was teetering on the very brink, rocking back and forth on unsafe ground with only life's goodwill holding him up. His face was overcast with sorrow, as if he was watching some unseen funeral in the spirit world passing before his eyes. His shoulders sagged so low they could hardly hold his head up. Each finger joint had stiffened as he tightened his grip ever harder on the chair. When the rain, too, had deserted him, his throat had become as parched as a sun-baked well. Gabriel Angélico was about to disintegrate beneath the heedless vault of the sky, while the world lay there before him and smiled back with indifference. Day and night he sat there, drinking rain-water, until his eyes started bleeding and his wits were about to be blown out of him.

For a long while she stood behind him contemplating his sorry form. So little remained of the Professor's lofty poise that Klara Jørgensen could hardly bear to look at him. Silently she began to cry, with a slight shaking of her shoulders and her hair like a threadbare backcloth covering her face. She went on with her quiet weeping, until her presence became coloured by a sunset that no one had quite seen the like of in this world of rock. Only when she'd managed to staunch her tears did she go over to the broken body before her and touch its neck. A sigh escaped from the Professor's mouth, before he quickly controlled himself and raised his head. They looked warily at one another for a moment, as if they were strangers. Then she gave way and glided down on to the unsteady chair by his side. For a moment she was certain everything was as before, that now they could sit here until morning came, then go home as usual. Afterwards, all her hurts would heal in the continuation of this. She would remain, she would go on returning so that never again would she have to know such a loss.

Gabriel Angélico felt his head becoming heavy and the sensation leaving his legs. He coughed suddenly and clutched his chest.

'You're ill, Professor,' said Klara Jørgensen.

'I've got a pain in my heart,' he replied.

She got up from her chair and bent down before him, lifted her glance to his tired eyes. Then she raised a hand and placed it on his breast, on his right breast, where his heart was leaping to and fro. How could she know? he thought dimly and opened his eyes wide for a moment, in the realisation that everything he'd believed in was true. She held her hand where it hurt most, over the spot where his heart had taken root all that time ago, when he was being shaped in his mother's womb. The pounding gradually eased and became an even tone, a comfort, a pain-reliever in itself.

'You've come to say goodbye,' he said.

'Yes,' she replied. 'But not for ever. I'll be back.'

Gabriel Angélico lifted his eyes to the line where sky and mountain met.

'Look at me,' she said resolutely and fixed her eyes on him. 'I'll be back.'

Two solid tears crept down his cheeks and she lifted her hand to wipe them away.

'Now come back down to earth with me,' she said, smiling.

Then they got up together and went back, each with a chair, over the mountains and across the river, to the house by the water's edge, where Mustafa lay praying in the reeds.

Gabriel Angélico told Klara Jørgensen about destiny. He told her how everyone is born under a star or a planet or, in some cases, a streak of lightning. He told her that the path a person treads is already carved out, like a fissure in a mountain-side, and that each individual has a kindred spirit they secretly search for. He told her how no one finds peace until they have discovered this kindred spirit, and so we human beings always go round in circles looking for the other half of ourselves. And Klara Jørgensen who'd never looked for anything at all, listened to him without understanding the meaning of it, but nodded all the same.

'I've waited for you all my life,' he said to her, just as he'd done once before.

'I know,' said Klara Jørgensen without further thought.

'I'll be back again. I'll be back before you've even got up from your chair, you'll see.'

'Are you going now?'

'Yes, I'm going.'

'I'll sit here till you come.'

'Soon. I'll come soon.'

She got up and stood before him. Gabriel Angélico hadn't the will power to rise. He hadn't the strength. Suddenly he was looking much older. Go now, he thought to himself and watched her cautiously. She smiled mournfully.

'Goodbye, Professor,' said Klara Jørgensen.

'Goodbye, Miss Klara,' said Gabriel Angélico.

Ana Risueña saw Klara Jørgensen disappear across the bridge and vanish into the darkness. The worldly-wise woman slid out from the doorway and took up position behind her son's bowed neck. He sat motionless under a bough laden with reluctant, bursting buds. It would have been hard to see that he was breathing, had it not been for the hand on his chest moving slowly up and down in time with his respiration. Ana Risueña brushed the sand from the steps and sat down with her legs stretched out on the dry gravel. She looked up for a moment to see if the girl could still be seen, but her outline had been devoured by the dusk. Total silence enveloped mother and son, as if a world no longer existed beyond the river-bank.

'Is she coming back?' asked Ana Risueña at last, her eyes fixed on the bridge.

'No,' replied Gabriel Angélico. 'She's gone with my life in her arms and won't ever be back.'

Klara Jørgensen stood on deck and watched the contours of Vidabella appear in the early morning light. Her senses were once again filled with the piercing cries of the pelicans and the rattle of chains on the quayside, the strong tang of salt and kelp. As she went ashore she was blinded by the sharp light she'd been unused to for so long and the heat that hugged the body like a damp cloak. She walked along the breakwater towing all her possessions behind her, as the sea-birds wheeled above her head and the keen air smarted against her cheeks. She had forgotten the smell of the sea, the way the waves offered themselves to the sand-banks, what it felt like to take off one's shoes and harden the feet. She had forgotten how the tightly packed bus-seats lulled her, how the wind along the highway was so welcome and so short-lived, how she would stretch her arms out of the window and try to draw it to her. She had forgotten how easy it was for someone to blot out the details of their own life, to relinquish one existence in favour of another as the days passed. The flat island landscape about her became real again, and with it a faint sense of belonging.

The small beach house seemed strangely unfamiliar and miraculously dear at the same time. She remembered it being larger; it looked as if it had shrivelled in the face of wind and weather during the four months she'd been away. The desk had been moved a little to the right to make room for a new house plant, a tall fern that stood in the shade by the window and hadn't yet been scorched by the sun. Her books were as she'd left them, but they had a thin covering of dust. Two new postcards were stuck to the fridge, both from her, with different mountain views. At one end of the kitchen unit hung a photo of the Penn family and she recognised the apple tree in the background. She wasn't in the picture. It had been taken before they'd met. She stood in the bedroom doorway and stared at the double bed, just as she'd done the first day she arrived. It no longer looked big, as it had done then. It, too, had shrunk. The bed was small and safe now, whereas the only things that seemed large in her world were the mountains out there and the secrets they harboured within them.

She took a bath in the cold water from the plastic tank and went out on to the veranda to dry herself in the wind. With only a thin dress on, she lay down in the hammock and was slowly rocked back and forth as she became sleepier and sleepier in the afternoon heat. Half dreaming, Klara Jørgensen realised that she'd never had problems going to sleep any-where, that she could doze off no matter where she laid her head. She'd never felt anxious about closing her eyes in totally unfamiliar surroundings. More difficult by far was finding peace when one was awake. Finding a place where one could enter into the spirit of the daily round and the conversations that constantly repeated themselves. For her, Santa Ana was just such a place. And as she was on the verge of sleep in the hammock, Klara Jørgensen felt it mattered little if she stayed in this tiny town for always. At the same time, it was a strange thought, because now more than ever she had a reason to leave it once again, and preferably sooner rather than later.

Some hours later she walked into Santa Ana as the town slumbered in the afternoon heat. The *empanadas* women had gone home, and the only thing that moved was the washing on the verandas, which barely rippled in the sea breeze. Klara Jørgensen wandered along the promenade, past a couple of dogs that had mated and were still struggling to uncouple, past the overfilled rubbish bins where a nest of kittens mewed amongst the left-overs, until she was again standing by the rickety tables of the shady restaurant where she had sat so many times before. Bianca Lizardi had fallen asleep in the kitchen doorway, with her strange thumb at an unnatural angle, while the fan above stroked her hair back from her moist forehead. The wallpaper had faded even more. The fringes on the bracket lamps had turned stiff in the sea air. Klara Jørgensen walked up to the railings at the end of the restaurant and leant on them and let the winds caress her face. Out there sailed her Captain. There he hauled on ropes, let himself be dried by the sun, prised open oysters with his knife and smiled at the people around him. She tried to recall his features, but they had faded after four months' absence.

She looked about for Ernest Reiser, but there was no sign of him anywhere. Perhaps he was having his customary soup at the Chinese eatery, and she was just about to go when Bianca Lizardi woke up and told her he was sleeping in his room. The waitress nodded towards the stairs and said emphatically that she ought to go and wake the old-timer, as he should have been down long before. Klara Jørgensen vacillated a moment; she'd never seen the old man's room, much less roused him from his siesta. She stole cautiously up the back stairs without noticing the spectacular view that made everyone pause on the top step. Finally she climbed the fire ladder until she stood on the roof of the building where the heat pounded on the dusty cement foundation. She'd had no inkling that there was anything up here on the roof of the town, and there wasn't a lot, other than some drooping clothes-lines and a small eminence with a door at one end. This, as it turned out, was the door to Ernest Reiser's room. She opened it gingerly and stepped across the threshold, ducking to avoid banging her hand on the lintel.

The room was oppressively hot. On the concrete floor in the corner nearest the door was a bucket of water, and a well-used bar of soap had slid towards the sluice in the floor. Further in, cracked Venetian blinds hung down over the window, and through them small shafts of light filtered in, highlighting the huge clouds of dust and fine sand that floated round the room. The only furniture was a bed without sheets and a wooden crate that had been turned upside down to serve as a bedside table. Ernest Reiser lay on the bed sleeping heavily, as sweat ran in silent streams from his face. His only covering was a damp cloth full of sweat marks. On the bedside table was the photo of a woman. She was young, pretty and smiling right into the camera with her hands resting in her lap. Her fingers were long and slender, her nails painted and her dress low-cut around her delicate shoulders. Klara Jørgensen could tell that the girl was happy. She could tell it because she herself must have worn a similar expression not so long ago. The sight of the girl made her feel embarrassed. She stood stiffly for a while and looked at the photograph with mistrust and a touch of fear. The sadness of life had descended on the room and was staring mutely at her from every corner. And just as she recognised that the feeling was no longer alien, a look of bitterness crept across her face and she closed the door quietly behind her.

Everything around her was as it had always been. Klara Jørgensen sat in the restaurant and read a book. On the table beside her a soft-green lemonade was slowly melting, and an ashtray stood as yet unused. She read in deep concentration, without allowing herself to be distracted by Umberto who now and again shot glances over her shoulder to find out what preoccupied her. Under the shade of the palm roof, Bianca Lizardi read her colourful magazines that fuelled the most unlikely dreams about her future. The fishermen trooped past one after the other with everything they hadn't managed to sell from the day's catch, closely followed by stray cats and a wayward gull or two. A couple of tourists came up from the beach and disappeared into the streets with travel guides and far too much money. A police constable slipped out from the building where Divina Fácil resided on the fourth floor, and checked in each direction before doing up his flies and driving off. Everything was as normal and Klara Jørgensen was left with the feeling that she'd never been away from this little patch of earth. She read on undisturbed as before, only occasionally raising her head to look towards the horizon and watch the sun's height above the line of the sea.

Ernest Reiser came downstairs and saw her sitting there. He gave a thin smile before pouring himself a glass of White Horse and filching a new packet of cigarettes from behind the bar. He'd only just put on a fresh shirt, but despite this his chest was already blotched with sweat marks, and he pulled his handkerchief out of his trouser pocket and mopped his face.

'Well, if it isn't young Miss Klara returned home again,' he said and came to sit opposite her.

'That's right,' she said and smiled.

'And has she come to stay?'

'We'll see.'

Ernest Reiser scanned the surface of the sea and cleared his throat with a little cough.

'Everything's just the same here.'

'And you, Ernie?'

'Just the same.'

They both squinted at the droplets of sun that were raining down into the mouth of the bay.

'And Miss Klara? How are things with her?'

Klara Jørgensen puckered her brow into small folds and didn't answer immediately.

'Is she just the same?' Ernest Reiser asked in the same tone of voice.

'No,' replied Klara Jørgensen with a slight shake of her head. 'No, I don't think so. I think something has happened to me.'

'And,' said the old man. 'What might that be?'

'I don't know,' she said.

Ernest Reiser smiled.

'Life. Life has happened to you. Sooner or later it does to everyone.'

He took a toothpick from his pocket and began to chew it, as he sighed gently. Klara Jørgensen leant forward slightly as she shaded her face with one hand.

'Ernie, why aren't you married any more?'

Ernest Reiser smiled with a certain abandonment.

'You see, Klara, love is so easy to make a mistake about.'

'Wasn't she the right person for you?' Klara Jørgensen asked round-eyed. The elderly man twisted one corner of his mouth into a smile and slowly shook his head.

'There is no right person. Or maybe there are hundreds of them. It's not love itself that's the problem, it's what we expect of it.'

The girl felt a smarting in her breast and screwed up her eyes a little against the evening sun. Ernest Reiser lit a cigarette as his eyes, too, narrowed.

'Love isn't some great, shining thing, I have to tell you, young Klara. It's just the sum of life's minute coincidences.'

The old man settled back in his chair and let out his third sigh in a very short space of time. Klara Jørgensen kept silent, but her eyes grew red, along with the sun. She knew now that she'd never see Gabriel Angélico again.

A familiar shadow approached on the horizon. A boat was sailing in. It looked small and shabby in the mouth of the bay, but grew into something known and dear as it got closer. As soon as she could glimpse the shapes of the people before the mast, Klara Jørgensen got up and walked towards the water's edge. She stepped carefully across the sun-baked sand and felt the wind stroking her hair. Her eyes contracted and she breathed more heavily, as if really she felt like crying. A figure slipped into the water and came wading in towards the shore with two red fish in his hand. He had cracks in his face and golden skin, great hands and an understanding look in his eyes.

There was so much about him to smile in remembrance over, and yet all of a sudden he seemed younger, as if the years that separated them had become insignificant, almost invisible.

A feeling of devotion spread from Klara Jørgensen's heart and into her breast like a small stitch. He still hadn't seen her. He was washing his feet at the water's edge and smiling at the group of tourists who were moving like a caravan of sunburnt bodies in towards land. Klara Jørgensen felt cold standing there and hugged her shoulders with her arms. For a moment she felt nauseous and in a cold sweat. He looked thinner. His shoulders were bowed and his arms, with those large hands like pendulums at the ends, hung loose. She moved slowly towards him, past the tables at the water's edge, but in short, unpreventable glimpses she kept seeing Gabriel Angélico's face under a parasol and had to blink and start again. Half way down she halted and buried her face in her hands. With one last effort she tried to erase all memories of the Professor who smiled at her with his hands in his pockets. She would never speak of him again, but if she did, she would refer to him simply as the Professor, as a stranger without a name. And perhaps she would be reduced in his memory to a student whom he'd once been a little too fond of. But a student, nothing more. That was how it must be. For just at that moment she'd made up her mind. She had found her place on earth. A person in whom to take up residence.

William Penn caught sight of the hunched figure under one of the white canvas parasols on the beach. He didn't recognise her immediately, but thought at first it was a stranger who was standing there crying. Only when a shaft of lilac-tinted light penetrated the shadow beneath the parasol did he see that it was Klara Jørgensen standing with her head in her hands, as if she were trying to squeeze all her thoughts out and shower them over the sand in front of her. He walked calmly over to her and stood before the small figure that was swaying slowly backwards and forwards. She peeped up through swollen eyes and saw that he was standing in front of her. And William Penn thought that perhaps the time had come to tell her he loved her. But words were just as difficult for the Captain now as they'd always been, so, instead, he put his arms around her in the belief that she needed a hug more than a well-formulated declaration of love. Klara Jørgensen heaved a sigh as she laid her head against the Captain's breast. She closed her eyes and breathed towards the soft thumping of the male heart within, gently hammering in her ear. And as William Penn held Klara Jørgensen tightly in his arms, she had the feeling that she had come home. A strange realisation, she admitted to herself, for she didn't feel that she'd been anywhere for such a very long time.

The Captain and his girl went to the tables in the restaurant and sat close together. They held hands and told one another stories, laughing or nodding softly across the table. They drank lemonade and smoked in their usual way as if no time had elapsed at all, and the only indication that they had been apart was the length of that evening's ritual. The sky was dark and sprinkled with stars, and the Captain's stomach rumbled so much that he padded off to Umberto in the kitchen to get himself something to eat. Afterwards he got talking in the bar briefly, and smiled at her with a small, hopeless roll of his eyes, as if to tell her that he hadn't changed much. And Klara Jørgensen smiled wanly, because the Captain was quite unable to see what life had done to her. It wasn't outwardly obvious. It wasn't even noticeable. He simply saw her as she'd always been and didn't realise that she'd emerged from her glasshouse and now inhabited the same perilous territory as himself. With a minute smile she lifted her book from the edge of the table and began to read slowly in the light from the bracket lamps. But it wasn't long before she put the story down again. Umberto came past and stopped in front of her as she sat watching the vanishing day.

'Don't you like it?' he asked, glancing at the book.

'It's beautiful,' she said. 'But incomprehensible.'

'Don't you understand it?' Umberto asked.

'No,' said Klara Jørgensen. 'And I'm not supposed to.'

Then she added with a little smile:

'It's magic.'

That last Christmas on Vidabella, Ernest Reiser taught her to make Venezuelan Christmas cakes. They were small, hard and took an age to shape. Klara Jørgensen thought they looked like eyes that glowered up at her from the baking tray, even though they gave off the most delightful smell. A year had passed since she'd left the mountains. She had returned to the daily routine she'd long since set for herself there, untaxing days of novels in the hammock, trips to the supermarket with her pink shopping net, a strong black coffee at the baker's, and finally the wait on the beach in the evening until she could make out the set of a sailing boat on the horizon. Likewise, she continued to cook for the Captain, clean the little beach house, change the oil in the car and fill up the plastic water tank, which she suspected of being leaky. So her days were filled with a whole list of little tasks which she performed with the greatest matter-of-factness. People who saw Klara Jørgensen in the streets of Santa Ana, carrying lemons and fish fillets, frying-bananas and maize flour, felt sure the girl was as happy as she looked. William Penn, too, thought she seemed content, much calmer now, as if she'd come to some sort of accommodation with life itself, a compromise between this quiet existence and a yearning that seemed to him sometimes to hollow out her expression. The Captain came to the conclusion that she was missing the mountains, that she had formed close friendships up there and had become very fond of this Señora Yolanda. But she spoke little of these intervening months and he let her keep her experiences to herself, just as he had allowed his to lie dormant in his own past.

Gabriel Angélico's name was never mentioned. No one suspected that young Klara had formed such an acquaintance. Nor did she ever think of writing to him, or telephoning, or asking after him during her sporadic chats with Señora Yolanda. With some reluctance Klara Jørgensen was forced to admit that the Professor's face was in the process of fading from her memory; the brown, mirthful eyes that had turned subdued when they were alone, the high cheek-bones and the dark skin, they all began to lose their detail and clarity, just as sandstorms hide the features of a landscape. Only his words continued to live within her, and she bore them like a claw in her breast. Sometimes it grew large, like the spines on a sea urchin, but it was never painful enough to make her cry. If she did harbour a wish to see him again, she was not allowed to admit it, not even to herself. And whereas in the beginning she'd thought of him night and morning and the memory of him lay like a sigh across her days, such moments gradually became filled with other activities. In the end, Gabriel Angélico's name had begun to mutate into a feeling she was only intermittently aware of, like the afterglow of a lovely thought.

Venezuelan Christmas cakes are far sweeter than Norwegian ones and sit heavily on the stomach. The taste of them drove away some of the longing Klara Jørgensen felt for a Christmas with her sister and parents, and was also better suited to the sultry Caribbean nights leading up to New Year. With moist hands, she folded the mixture and added the necessary ingredients that Ernest Reiser had laboriously measured out. When all was well mixed, the old man took out a jar of small, rough nuts and as soon as he removed the lid, a faint, alluring scent wafted into the room. With wrinkled fingers he pressed the nuts against a grater and rasped them into a deep bowl, and the smell grew in strength.

'Nutmegs,' said Ernest Reiser, smiling almost secretively at the girl.

'Is that what they look like?' said Klara Jørgensen, entranced.

'Have you never seen them before, Klara?'

'Not like this, not before they've been grated.'

'This is the secret,' said Ernest Reiser. 'One must preserve the taste until the last moment.'

She breathed in the smell from the bowl and her senses reeled at what they encountered.

'It has quite a bitter after-taste, but gives off the most wonderful smell,' said Ernest Reiser.

Gingerly, she took a pinch of the ground nut and sprinkled it over the cake mixture.

'Go steady, now,' Ernest Reiser warned. 'It's like a drug.'

'Really?' said Klara Jørgensen, opening her eyes wide.

'Absolutely. You get quite hooked. Either that, or it makes you ill.'

'Is that so?'

'Yes,' said Ernest Reiser as a serious look stole across his face.

'Nutmeg should only be consumed in very small quantities.'

And Klara Jørgensen nodded obediently, for she was well aware that the old man had been around long enough to know a thing or two about baking.

Two days later Ernest Reiser was hit by a car as he crossed the road near the beach. His worn body was hurled towards one of the promenade's marble benches and lay motionless amongst wind-blown rubbish and *tigua* seed. The packet of cigarettes he'd just bought from Rafael el Grande burst as he fell, and for an instant there was a shower of Blue Belmonts, before they fell like large matches to the pavement, white as the war graves on the French Atlantic coast. The car which had struck Ernest Reiser in the side was from the police headquarters at Puerto de las Naves, and the man driving it was a policeman. The accident took place at five in the afternoon, at a time when a hush had descended on the town and the shops dozed. It was later found that both Ernest Reiser and the officer were well over the limit when the collision occurred. As soon as he heard the sharp bang, Rafael el Grande slowly raised his head, as he often did when stray dogs were run over, giving a final yowl on their way into the dark jaws of death. With a soft sigh he watched the people gathering about the lifeless old man, before he turned to the telephone and dialled an ambulance. Then he rang Henrik Branden, who had just poured himself his first rum on the veranda, glad to have arrived at the day's better end.

'Death has driven past and caught Ernest Reiser in the side,' Rafael el Grande said into the phone.

'Is he alive?'

'I don't know. But he's finished anyway.'

153

'What do you mean, you rogue?'

'If he doesn't die here, he'll die in the hospital.'

'You can't be certain of that.'

'Oh yes. Yes, I can,' said Rafael el Grande and replaced the phone.

Then he turned to the door and looked out at the little gathering of people and shook his head.

'There are two places you should always avoid in this country,' he mumbled to himself. 'Prison and hospital.'

Klara Jørgensen sat on the stained concrete floor of the Hospital Louis Ortega, beneath a bluish light. At the other end of the corridor, Henrik Branden was having constant conversations on his mobile phone. The smell of disease was there just as it was in the hospitals at home, but here there were no beds on wheels, no drugs trolleys or sanitary wipes, no white sheets. The doctors at Louis Ortega, ineffectual and lacking resources, didn't walk, they ran. Once the sleek vein on a patient's neck had ceased to throb, they gave a quick sigh and straightened the bed so that another poor creature could take their turn. Outside these torrid rooms whole families sat and waited for a loved one who was swimming about in the depths of coma. They sat with knitting and domino boards and passed the hours, ate dry biscuits and chewed meekly, drank water from dusty plastic bottles, not sure whether to cover themselves in sorrow or write the whole thing off as part of the fickleness of life.

Through the acoustics of confusion, Klara Jørgensen heard Henrik Branden speaking to a young doctor. Though he pulled out his stuffed wallet and waved crinkled notes, it made no difference. The young doctor merely shrugged his shoulders and nodded towards the private clinic across the road. Henrik Branden snapped his wallet shut with a resigned twitch of his shoulders and walked over to Klara Jørgensen's hunched form to give her a fistful of notes.

'This is for medicine,' he said.

'What sort?' she asked.

'Antibiotics. And something to deaden the pain.'

'What about water?'

'Buy some water as well. And a couple of pairs of underpants.'

The girl felt her chest filling, like a sponge that has been laid in water.

'The private clinic,' was all she managed to blurt out.

'It would cost fifty thousand,' he interrupted.

'Bolívares?'

'Kroner.'

Henrik Branden shook his head.

'He's an old man,' was all he said.

Klara Jørgensen looked away. She crumpled the notes in her hand and pushed them into her pocket, before marching out to join the queue of people at the pharmacy on the other side of the street.

Ernest Reiser lay on a rusty iron bed with his legs apart. The walls of the room were shiny and oozed small rivulets of plaster, while the windows gaped on to the street and tried to catch any vestige of breeze that might come. Bianca Lizardi had brought the old man a sheet that had already become creased and soaked. Ernest Reiser's mouth was open and he was gazing out into the room, although one eye was bandaged over. The eye was crushed, the doctors said, but an operation could possibly save his sight. His right arm had been put in plaster immediately and from time to time the old man let out a low groan and clutched it, as if it itched frantically. One tube had been inserted into Ernest Reiser's lung and he urinated through another. Bianca Lizardi sat tirelessly at his bedside and tried to give the patient liquid by pressing moistened cotton wool against the teeth. Sweat ran from Ernest Reiser's greyish-white hair and the droplets collected in the deep folds of skin, like small pools of water in a rough hillside. Klara Jørgensen thought he looked incalculably old, wizened and on his way out of the ranks of the living; and yet, in the morning light, he was like a small child before going to bed in the evening, waiting for the fairytale before the light is unwillingly turned out.

For endless days they waited, paralysed by the caring instinct the old man kindled in them all. Klara Jørgensen sat on the floor in a corner, her back against the white walls, heedless of the passage of time. Only after it had long grown dark would she return home to sleep, uneasy and disturbed by the sea's hungry dance, but next morning she'd be there again, in the morose corridors, on the smooth, dazzling floor. Bianca Lizardi sat unsleeping by his bedside day and night, keeping vigil over the old man. Carmen de la Cruz and Henrik Branden were always turning up with more money and William Penn also filled Klara Jørgensen's pockets with cash every morning. And she continued to buy every possible medicine, crisply pressed sheets, litre bottles of water and pairs of pants in children's sizes. Some mornings she'd arrive to find them all stolen, and then she'd use her own money to replace the items. From time to time the doctors made fleeting visits, talked anxiously about the condition of his eye and then went away again.

Sometimes Klara Jørgensen sat holding the old man's hand, laid her delicate fingers round the bony hands covered in skin that looked as if someone had thrust an oversized pair of leather gloves on them. It was with a certain reluctance that she looked at his skeletal body through the folds in the sheet, the flabby breast and the sunken cheeks. He lay there quite helpless, gasping for air, rambling incoherently about fishing trips from his childhood and the pelicans' suicide, before dozing off with a little whimper. Klara Jørgensen remembered the man in Ernest Reiser's old passport, the gentleman he'd once been, the man of charisma who had felt himself invincible at times. And yet there he lay, vanquished by life, and at times Klara Jørgensen couldn't bear to see him like that, but had to sit out in the corridor and catch her breath for a while. She wasn't like Bianca Lizardi, who wiped away the spit that ran from the corner of his mouth, who emptied the bucket that his urine went into, who washed the exhausted body and wiped his malodorous brow with a cool cloth. Occasionally Klara Jørgensen would look with wonder at the waitress because of the matter-of-fact way that she performed these services.

'It's wonderful, what you're doing, Bianca,' said Klara Jørgensen.

Bianca Lizardi simply shrugged her shoulders and attempted to change the old man's underpants without staring too much.

'He's alone, like me,' she replied.

The old man complained incessantly about the pain in his

plastered arm. It was difficult to tell if he'd lost his wits, or merely wept because he'd finally realised the condition he was in. But the screams from his parched throat were driving Klara Jørgensen mad. Each day she implored the doctors to change the plaster, but there was no money for that, they told her. So she bought the necessary supplies from the chemist and wheedled again, to no avail. Ernest Reiser continued to howl like a bleeding baboon. Finally, Klara Jørgensen could stand these helpless cries no longer; she stood with clenched fists before the bed, as if for an instant she'd considered beating the old man to death. Instead, she went to him, took a pair of scissors from his bedside table and carefully cut away the plaster until it fell away like a dry scab. Klara Jørgensen staggered back as the wound revealed itself. Gasping, she averted her face from the sharp stink of putrefaction that emanated from it, but, unable to grasp what she had seen, she looked again at the old man's arm. Ernest Reiser's wound was full of fly larvae groping aimlessly about, smooth and shiny in all their horror, as they ate away at the red human flesh. She stood staring at them, her chest gurgling and her eyes swelling. Then she started weeping silently, and began to remove the larvae one by one, throwing them on the floor and crushing them until they turned into a greyish mush beneath her shoes. Her efforts had little effect, there were too many of them, and in the end she couldn't bear the accompanying stench. So she went out of the room and caught sight of a young doctor who happened to be chasing up the corridor with his coat fluttering behind him like a bridal train.

'You forgot to clean it,' Klara Jørgensen said to him, her voice flat.

'Sorry?' said the doctor, halting.

The girl tugged at his arm and pulled him into the room where the old man lay.

'You forgot to clean the wound,' she said, fighting back spasms of sobs in her throat. Instead she sank to the floor next to him with her face in her hands.

'Clean it, please. I implore you,' she whispered to the doctor, who went out quickly and called two sisters from the other end of the corridor. The three of them began to clean Ernest Reiser's devoured arm, turning their heads away from the ghastly smell. Klara Jørgensen sat by the bed and cried. Perhaps in that moment she was crying for all that was lamentable in this world, all the hopelessness that existed and all her private store of despair. But her shoulders exhibited no seething convulsions of betrayal. On the contrary, all that could be heard was an empty and silent sorrow which makes no great fuss, but which hurts as it fights its way out of the body.

Ernest Reiser was wheeled into the operating theatre of the Louis Ortega together with a woman in labour and a child with appendicitis. Henrik Branden had laid out fifteen thousand Norwegian kroner on the table before the hospital management, and an artificial eye was to be fitted. With a transparent sheet over the lower part of his body, Ernest Reiser was trundled through the hospital corridors on a mobile bed with a small posse following behind. William Penn had also come that day to see the old chap before they deprived him of his consciousness. Just before he was taken into the operating theatre, Ernest Reiser looked round the little group, as if a final remnant of cynical self-irony were about to emerge. But he must have decided it wasn't worth the trouble of leaving them with well-formulated words of wisdom. In addition, as they all suspected, he might well have been mad. But as they waited for the doors to open, Ernest Reiser touched Klara Jørgensen's waist and tugged at the sleeve of her blouse. The girl bent down and felt the sick, febrile breath hit her in the face.

'What is it, Ernie?' she asked.

'The pelicans,' said Ernest Reiser.

'Yes, I know,' she said.

At that moment the old man's eyes filled with tears, he looked round with a measure of desperation and smiled wanly at the girl in front of him. Klara Jørgensen was filled with sadness, too, because it was as if the mists before his eyes had lifted, and he saw himself moving towards death, waving farewell as the white handkerchief of life shook out all the experiences of his years.

'You know what I like best?' said the old man.

'No, Ernie,' Klara Jørgensen replied.

'Whisky,' said Ernest Reiser. 'With crushed ice and a splash of water. Life's a torrid business. You need something to cool it down with.'

Ernest Reiser died of hepatitis B a week later and was buried beneath the mango trees in the Santa Ana cemetery. A surprising number of people turned up for the funeral. They tried to cool their faces with fans bearing pictures of Spanish matadors. Henrik Branden spoke a short eulogy for the old man, who seemed to be without homeland or family, but not without friends on this island where he'd spent his final years.

With her hands clasped and her head bowed, Klara Jørgensen stood thinking how strange it all was, that these people who'd only known Ernest Reiser when life had already begun its farewell song to him, were the ones to bid him a last goodbye. All the others who'd been part of his life in one way or another were gone, were somewhere else. Perhaps they couldn't even recall who Ernest Reiser from Geneva, Caracas and Vidabella really was. A pale remembrance, perhaps. A flicker from a failing memory. But when the funeral was over, Klara Jørgensen caught sight of a woman wearing a headscarf who was standing in the shade of a forget-me-not over by the wall, some distance from the rest of the cortège. Her coat was faded and of indeterminate colour, her eyes looked as if they were on a slow journey down her face, and her hands shook a little. She wasn't crying, and gave no indication that she felt anything at that moment, but she stared a long time at the coffin, which had become decorated with a ripe fruit of some kind that had fallen and splattered on the lid.

At the end of the ceremony Klara Jørgensen went tentatively up to the woman and asked gently:

'Are you his wife?'

The woman looked up in surprise, with a tired expression.

'Yes. That's right.'

'My condolences, then.'

The woman pulled back the corners of her mouth a little and rubbed her hands.

'I hardly ever saw him. So does it sound strange if I say I'm going to miss him?'

'Not in the least,' said Klara Jørgensen.

'He was always there, you see,' said the woman.

'And you didn't even get the chance to say goodbye.'

The woman smiled softly, as if shrouded in a beautiful memory.

'We said goodbye all the time,' she said. 'It was always the last thing we said.'

'He was really fond of you.'

'As I was of him.'

'It was such a pity you couldn't share a home,' said Klara Jørgensen with a certain degree of wonder.

The woman smiled faintly.

'Those you love aren't necessarily the ones you're best suited to live with.'

'No,' said Klara Jørgensen, nodding. 'I know that only too well.'

She took the woman's hands and squeezed them gently, before leaving the burial ground with the Captain's arm about her waist. The all-too-great love of Ernest Reiser's life stood a long time before his grave. Passers-by saw her stand there until evening, with her hands clasped and her face veiled in pensiveness. The next morning she was gone.

Klara Jørgensen and William Penn left Vidabella three weeks later, with suitcases full of conch shells, red-scorched sand from the great savannahs in the south and two bottles of Venezuelan rum. They scrubbed their way out of the small beach house, until the smell of soap was everywhere, while the postcards on the fridge were thrown away, along with a home-made Advent calendar manufactured from matchboxes and glittery, red paper. The pot-plants were given to Bianca Lizardi in the certain knowledge that they would wither away before the summer was over, as the waitress had no feeling for flowers whatsoever. Umberto bid the young couple farewell with a jar of octopus in vinegar and olive oil, and a baleful face, as if the dullness of the evenings would now be complete. The bed-linen was given away as well, together with the towels, the pots and pans, the cracked crockery and the cutlery, which was minus two teaspoons, as happens in the best of families that have lived in a place for any length of time. Return dates were stamped on their tickets, the taxi was ordered, and people at home were warned that Klara Jørgensen and William Penn were on their way back. The old Malibu car was taken over by Henrik Branden and Carmen de la Cruz. The sailing boat was sold to a Dutch tourist, who'd fallen in love with the little island – it was so lovely and hot here and there was so much to drink, it was sheer paradise. With the gleam of boyish dreams in his eyes, he was handed the papers, while William Penn signed without further ado or hint of regret. At last, the Captain put up the shutters of the beach house and packed up his hammock, which daily use and the sea winds had worn out. Early one morning the pair finally left the island on which they'd spent two years together, got into a taxi with rattling door-handles and sunken seats, and drove to the airport on Vidabella's windswept north coast, without looking back once.

Many years later, just after she'd given birth to her first child, Klara Jørgensen sat thinking that autumn had become rather a dreary event. She was no longer so captivated by it. It merely reminded her that time was passing, creeping on and adding another line or two to her face. Similarly, she noticed that the Captain was looking older too. He'd passed forty and didn't go sailing as much as he had done. But he still went about with a content and tranquil expression on his face, as if his half-lived life had given him more than he had a right to expect. She felt content as well, perhaps even happy, the sort of happiness that lies smouldering from day to day, but which occasionally flares up into a tenacious glow. The Captain and his girl were married now. The wedding had been held in one of Oslo's many churches one early autumn day with the entire family present. Leonora Bigotti had cried her face stripey and waved energetically as they set off on their honeymoon to the Italy of her childhood. Then another summer arrived and with it a little boy with dark eyes and light blond hair – a rather unusual combination, according to the midwife. And Klara Jørgensen sat at the kitchen window with the little one in her arms and saw the leaves creeping along the pavement as they crumbled slowly away, a sure sign that the years were passing, that she was getting older, no girl any more, but a perfectly ordinary woman and mother.

During the six years that had passed since they'd come home from the Caribbean, they had never considered going back. Holidays were instead filled with destinations closer at hand – a summer in Provence, a winter in Salzburg, a late spring in Pamplona. The summer after their son was born, they took him with them to the Greek islands, wandered round with the pram through narrow, marble-covered streets with the blue sea forming a thrilling backdrop behind them. They dozed with the other tourists on the beach, ate late breakfasts in the village below the hotel, took the bus round the islands with the child in their lap and shared a meal or two with the parents of other toddlers. It was one evening when they were having dinner in a little garden by a whitewashed church that Klara Jørgensen felt a sort of memory returning to her, triggered by the sight of a stray cat trying to fish a cockroach out of a rusty bucket. She knew again the taste of olives, over-ripe fruit and sweet liquor, mixed with the scent of the flower pollen that fell heedlessly to the ground. She felt the charged air caress the skin like a cradle-song, and she peered down at her own skin, golden and slightly red, as it had been then. Was it really so long ago? Had she forgotten everything? She looked at the Captain who was feeding their son with a teaspoon on the other side of the table. And it struck her that he no longer looked like a captain of any kind, but just like any other father in a short-sleeved shirt and light trousers, with a mildly sunburnt brow. A person who suddenly seemed remarkably ordinary, as humdrum as their days had steadily grown.

When their son turned five, the Jørgensen and Penn families gathered for a birthday party at Klara Jørgensen's in-laws' house at Bomannvik. It was mid-summer, Leonora Bigotti had got her strawberries to ripen by singing to them and they sat eating in the garden on white-painted benches. As coffee was being served, Klara Jørgensen's mother began to talk about her daughter's own birth, which had almost taken place in northern Italy. By some miracle, however, they'd managed to make it home, her mother reminisced, so that little Klara could come to the world in the Norwegian capital. Mind you, not under a star, as so many people insist. No, Klara Jørgensen was born beneath a flash of lightning. Even the hospital's own records had noted the event.

'That was quite something,' said Leonora Bigotti enthusiastically. 'How many people in the world can say they were born just as lighting strikes the earth?'

And it was at this oblique remark that the thirty-year-old Klara Jørgensen went quickly up to her in-laws' bedroom, locked the door and burst into tears, while no one could say for certain what or whom she was crying for.

His name was Gabriel Angélico and he was born with his heart on the right. All his life he'd lived in the same town, in the same house, in the same invisible speck on the world atlas. In later years he was always to be seen sitting on a chair of plaited plastic under the olive tree by the river where he lived. Here he would sit and watch the sun sinking over the lip of the mountains before him, with an expression of yearning on his face. Now and then the people of this neighbourhood noted that the good Professor had become even more introverted than they could ever remember him being. But maybe that wasn't so strange; after all, what had become of that foreign girl? Ana Risueña simply shook her head and replied that she had come and then gone again, like girls often do. During the day the Professor taught as before, although his sorrow-stamped face didn't elicit the same degree of merriment as of old. In time he also began to feel a mysterious pain in his body, which rapidly grew so unbearable that he couldn't work any more. In despair, Gabriel Angélico visited one doctor after another, and learnt that certain of his internal organs were moving about and that now, unfortunately, it was too late to do anything about it. Instead, Gabriel Angélico seated himself on the chair in front of the house where he lived and remained sitting thus, for countless days, with his hand on the right side of his breast, a trifle dopey from the analgesics he'd been prescribed and on which he'd gradually become totally reliant.

At the age of thirty-eight Professor Angélico died in the chair he had so thoroughly worn out with the weight of his bent body. He slipped away one morning to a fireworks display of sunbeams and it was to be many hours before anyone noticed that his heart beat no more. Eventually they managed to get him into the living-room and lay him out on the sofa, while they waited for the university hospital to come and claim his broken-down body. Only when his papers were brought out was it realised that the Professor had altered his will. His body wasn't to be bequeathed to the hospital now, as he'd originally intended, but was to be cremated instead. His ashes were to be strewn on the Caribbean Sea, on a day when the wind was blowing towards the north. Ana Risueña knitted her brows at her son's peculiar request, but saw to it that he was cremated and put into an urn. Only Victor Alba shook his head and said he thought his grandson had been mad if he thought they would all traipse off to the coast to wave him on his way into death. Water was water, his grandfather insisted, and sprinkled Gabriel Angélico's remains on the river below the house instead. There the neighbourhood women fluttered their embroidered handkerchiefs as a thin veil of ash blew out across the green water to be borne away by the currents. Some small particles of ash were caught up by the wind and no one could say for sure how far they travelled before they came to earth. But perhaps one or two eventually made it all the way to the sea, as Gabriel Angélico himself had yearned to do all his life. Out there, invisible, brittle flakes of ash were hurled down into the waves and drifted aimlessly onwards on a ridge of white foam, just as small human lives are tossed back and forth to the impatient heartbeat of the universe.